THE REA

ADVERSE CITY

Book 1

BONITA & HODGE

COVER DESIGN BEN HARRIS

THE REAL HOUSEWIVES OF
ADVERSE CITY
BOOK 1

BY

SHELIA E. BELL

ISBN-13: 978-1530302659
ISBN-10: 153030265X

Printed in the United States of America

Library of Congress Control Number: 2016903776

This is a work of fiction. Names, characters, places, and incidents either are products of the author's imagination or are used fictitiously. Any resemblance to actual events or locales or persons, living or dead, is entirely coincidental.

Acknowledgements

I always have to say *thank you* to my literary supporters, to those who take the time to purchase and read my books. This journey I'm on is one that I had no idea would transpire in my life. It's absolutely mind boggling how God orchestrates and directs our lives. My writing career was birthed out of tragedy. Who would have thought out of the darkest time of my life that God was about to do a new thing in me, through me, and for me.

I thank every book club, every friend and acquaintance, past and present, who contributed to my literary dreams. Thank you to my family, my amazing sons (Kevin, Jr., included), and to my mother who shower me with unconditional love and acceptance.

Thank you to Lacricia A'ngelle and Regina Dobbins for editing and proofreading my work. Thank you for taking the time to make sure that what I write is the best story possible.

Finally, but definitely not least, I give ALL praises, honor, and glory to God for loving me and for making me his Amazing Girl. There is No me without YOU, Lord.

God's Amazing Girl,
Shelia

"Every adversity, every failure, every heartache, carries with it the seed of an equivalent or greater benefit."
Napoleon Hill

Chapter 1

"Real friends don't get offended when you insult them. They smile and call you something even more offensive." Unknown

"Girl, I don't know how you do it," Avery said, stirring the lemon in her flavored seltzer water.

"Do what?" asked Meesha, sipping on a virgin lime margarita. The sun was high, and the breeze from the Florida coastline swayed her Brazilian weave from side to side.

"You know what I'm talking about; deal with all of those hoochies at the church pawing all over Pastor Porter."

"Don't mind Avery," Peyton said, sucking down her second full strength Vodka martini.

"I pray about it and go about my business. I can't live my life distrusting my husband. Besides, I keep myself fit and fabulous for him. Those so-called, uh, what are they called today?"

"THOTS," Peyton answered quickly.

"Those THOTS don't stand a chance." Meesha laughed, throwing her head back, revealing her flawless figure.

"Four kids, you're doing more than staying fit and fabulous. Sounds like you keeping him happy between the sheets, too," Eva, a native of Bolivia, said in her thick Spanish accent. She pushed back her long, flowing, thick black hair from off her face. Hair that women like Meesha paid for.

The four housewives sat on the outside patio of one of Adverse City, Florida's most exclusive restaurants, dining on some of the best foods and drinks in the city.

Adverse City, a quaint town was tucked between Fisher Island and Miami Beach, with homes of the rich and famous lining the white sandy beaches of the Atlantic Coastline. The temperature hovered most of the time between 70-80 degrees.

"Anyway, I have too many other things to deal with besides worrying about what woman is chasing after Carlton. I'm secure in our marriage. I've given him four sons and this body can give him more kids, if that's what he wants."

"Girl, please. You better sit yourself down somewhere." Peyton finished off her vodka martini and beckoned their server. "I'll have a cosmopolitan this time."

Yes, ma'am," the male server stated. He left and moments later returned with her drink.

Peyton lifted the glass to her lips and scoured. "Take this back," she told the server before he had time to leave her table. "Tell the bartender to fix me a *real* drink, top shelf! I don't taste a hint of vodka in this."

"I apologize, ma'am. I'll bring you another one."

Meesha, Eva, and Avery laughed as the young man scurried away from the table.

"What's so funny?" asked Peyton.

"You. Girl, you had that young boy so scared, I thought he was going to pee in his pants," cracked Avery.

The young server returned with another drink. Peyton tasted it, looked at him, and nodded her approval. He smiled and looked pleased then turned and walked away.

"Seriously, you need to hold back on the liquor, girlfriend. The day is still long," advised Meesha.

"I can handle my own. These drinks are nothing more to me than what you're drinking."

"Okay, whatever. But, you're the one always crying about your weight. I'm just saying, liquor adds fat and calories to your waistline."

"Just because you're skin and bones, don't eat meat, and don't drink liquor, don't try to judge me."

"I'm not trying to judge you. I'm just saying, you're the one who's always the first to cry about being overweight."

"Whatever, Meesha." Peyton flung her blonde locks back off her face and threw up one hand.

"Now ladies, ladies," Avery interjected. "We're here to enjoy what's supposed to be our girls' day out. It's supposed to be fun and relaxing. You know how hectic all our schedules are, and it's not often that we can get together for some girl time. Don't blow it with all of this female bickering. We are not like those TV housewives."

"Avery's right. I have enough drama in my life on a daily basis. When I'm with my girls, I don't want to hear all of this ying yang," added Eva.

Peyton rolled her blue eyes in her head and took another swallow of her cosmopolitan.

"Tell us what's going on with you and Ryker. I saw on CNN that he was representing that NFL player who was accused of giving some stupid girl that went up to his hotel room, the date rape drug."

"Some of these women out here need to get somewhere and sit down," Meesha said.

"They act like they don't understand what they're getting into when they agree to go to a hotel room with a man just because he's rich and famous," Avery said.

"I think they're no different from a prostitute," Eva stated.

"I agree with you, but that still doesn't give him the right to drug her. If she's willing to go to his room, she was probably going to give up the cookies anyway. All

3

he had to do was play his cards right. He was just as stupid," Peyton added, as she turned up the cosmopolitan and took her last swallow. She followed up by tracing her lips with her tongue like she was trying to savor the taste of the mixed drink for as long as she could.

"Anyway, since you all are so nosy, and always wanting to know about me and Ryker, let me assure you that we've never been better." Avery's eyes flitted over the faces of each of her friends. Each of them looked genuinely attentive to what she was saying about her recently troubled marriage.

'That was quick," Peyton said and chuckled.

Avery gave Peyton a raised eyebrow and then kept on talking. "I think Ryker and I are finally back on track. I know things were rough this past year, but I love my man, and I'm not about to give up on my marriage."

Meesha spoke up while she used her fork to play around in her garden salad. "God is in the business of making crooked places straight, which is why I had no doubt he would heal your marriage."

"Good for you, and for Ryker too, if he realizes that he almost lost a good woman." Eva frowned slightly. "I mean, I don't know if I could have been as strong as you if I discovered Harper cheated on me. It's just too much."

"I'm not saying it was easy. Quite the opposite; it was tough, real tough. I thought I was going to lose my mind when I found out he was cheating. Then you know that skank didn't have any morals whatsoever. You would think that she would have realized that he wasn't going to leave a wife and two young children."

"Most married men never leave their wives for the other woman," said Meesha. "She's a lawyer, just like Ryker. Seems like she would have had enough smarts to know that."

4

"Obviously, she didn't," Avery said. "I guess she really had the notion that sleeping with the head of Ryker and Klein Law firm would help her make partner. Instead, what she got was humiliated and pushed out the door."

"Probably because Ryker realized if he kept screwing around that he was going to lose you and his girls," Peyton told her.

"Not only that," Meesha said, "you could have taken his butt to the cleaners and left him high and dry."

"I know that's right," Eva said. "Girl, if that had been Harper, he wouldn't have a law firm or anything else."

All the ladies laughed.

"I agree," Peyton added. "Hey," she called out as the server walked pass their table. She lifted her glass toward him. "I'll have another one."

The server nodded in response.

"You need help," said Avery.

"She needs prayer," Meesha corrected.

"Look, I don't need help or prayer. I have this under control. Now I wish you all would get off my back."

The ladies continued their conversation, laughing, exchanging updates, reveling in their ultra-rich lives.

Chapter 2

"Love is when he gives you a piece of your soul that you never knew was missing." T. Tasso

Eva slowly turned over in the custom-made double king sized bed. Her eyes opened at the same time she eased her perfectly sculptured body next to her husband, only to fully open her eyes and see that once again she was in the bed alone. She stretched out her arm and ran it up and down the cold Egyptian cotton sheets.

How much more did he expect her to take? Harper rarely came home before midnight and left their home most mornings before five a.m. She understood being the Chief Medical director at Adverse General Hospital and a well-respected cardiovascular surgeon demanded a lot of his time. As if that wasn't enough, twice divorced, Harper's multi-millionaire status was also due to him being the author of several bestselling medical books, and for seven years he hosted his own award winning TV medical show. Now that he had stepped away from his TV show, he devoted his time to Adverse General hospital.

Eva was young, just twenty-nine years old, and she wanted a life, a real life. She thought Harper was the man who would make all of her fairy tale dreams come true. Sure, he was a great provider; whatever she wanted or thought she wanted, he had no problems making sure she got it, except for one thing: *him.* He was never around, they rarely spent time together, and their sex life was all but null and void. Something had to give.

She and Harper had been married for almost three years. He was ten years her senior with a twenty-three year old son named Seth who Harper fathered when he was only sixteen years old. He married Seth's mother when the couple turned eighteen, but the marriage slowly unraveled as Harper's education took precedence over his marriage and family.

Eva wanted to give Harper a baby too, but he told her that he wanted to wait until he had more time to devote to raising another kid. Eva reluctantly agreed, but what she hadn't agreed to was spending her days and nights alone. Harper encouraged her to get involved in things that she was interested in, that she gave him credit for. He wasn't the jealous type but sometimes Eva wished that he was; then maybe he would give her a little more of his undivided attention.

The fact that she didn't work a nine to five added to her frustration of being all alone in an oversized house, except for the company of her three Yorkshire terriers and the hired help. She looked at the foot of the bed and all three of the pooches were huddled together fast asleep.

Eva sat up in the bed and the three little pooches simultaneously woke up. Hopping across the bed, they were all over her, giving her sloppy kisses on her face and neck.

She petted each of them while alternating between speaking in her native tongue and English as she talked doggie talk to them.

Eva was often told she heavily resembled the Mexican singer Paulina Rubio. Granted, like the singer, it was difficult at times to understand Eva because her accent was so pronounced.

Eva, poured love on her doggies one more time before she stretched and got out of the bed. After taking a long hot bath, which she preferred over taking showers, she dressed and went downstairs to the kitchen where she made herself a boiled egg, a slice of wheat toast, and a glass of grapefruit juice. She fed the dogs and after they finished eating, she gathered their leashes from the mudroom and got them ready for their daily morning walk.

Eva walked a mile every morning along the walking trails inside their gated community. Peyton and Avery lived in the same community and Meesha lived in another private community about seven miles east.

When she finished her walk, she sat down on one of the benches in the dog park, removed the leashes off the pooches, and let them run around with several other dogs that frequented the private park.

Ding. Her text message notifier chimed. She removed the smartphone from its pouch on her side and looked down at it. It was Harper.

"Hope u njoy ur day sweetheart. I love u."

Eva smiled. Harper was really a great guy. She didn't want to sound like the unappreciative wife, but it was hard to go day after day, week after week without love and affection from her husband, other than his text messages and the lavish gifts he showered her with. All of that was well, but it didn't satisfy the physical ache of being touched, caressed, and made love to by her man.

"I love you 2. R u comin home early tonight?" she texted back.

"Not sure. I'll try, but if u hve plans keep them."

"I miss u. I woke up this morning and u weren't next to me. I need u, baby."

"I miss u too. I promise I'll make it up to u."

Eva understood right away what that meant. She could expect a few dozen roses or another diamond bracelet or piece of jewelry, but that didn't satisfy her sexual needs, or her desire to spend time with the man she loved. She didn't want to admit it, but she was beginning to realize why his other two marriages may have failed.

"Going to b a long day. Love u. gotta go," Harper texted.

Harper was strong in his faith and his belief in God was unshakeable. They met each other when he visited Bolivia three years prior as a medical missionary. He was part of a missionary group called Matters of the Heart. They were a group made up of Christian doctors and heart surgeons that freely performed heart surgery on some of Bolivia's poorest. Eva worked for pennies as a part-time receptionist at the community center turned makeshift hospital where doctors and their medical staff performed a variety of medical procedures on the country's poor.

Harper's thick black eyebrows, broad shoulders, cinnamon toast complexion, and winning smile won her over the moment he approached her counter. He was drop dead gorgeous and her heart seemed to skip a beat, maybe two, when he introduced himself and asked for her help in finding where he and his staff were to set up. That day was the beginning of a whirlwind courtship. Harper remained in Bolivia for three and a half weeks. By the time he finished his mission work, he and Eva had become a couple. Almost every night, at the end of his shift, the two of them were together. He made her laugh and she helped him improve his Spanish vocabulary. Some days, after work, she would prepare him and his staff dishes of her favorite Bolivian delights. Cooking happened to be something she was extremely good at. She had thought about becoming a chef but coming from a poor family, she decided against it and instead worked any job she could to help support her parents and her younger brother and sister. She had another brother who was a year older then she was, and much like Eva, he did whatever he could to help support the family. Her parents worked hard for very little money.

"God, how much longer do you expect me to do this?" she prayed and looked up toward heaven as she stood in front of the floor to ceiling kitchen window. The day was absolutely gorgeous. The weather was perfect, and the sun was shining bright but inside she felt like her light was dim and her heart was growing heavy. What was a girl to do?

Chapter 3

"Love recognizes no barriers. It jumps hurdles, leaps fences, penetrates walls to arrive at its destination full of hope." Maya Angelou

Meesha got up to prepare for sunrise devotion. It was a daily ritual for her. Every morning, like clockwork, she rose from her bed at 5:30 a.m. Carlton was already up and in his study preparing to share a daily message with those who called in on a regular basis to listen to his devotional followed by a prayer and his blessing on his faithful followers.

Meesha dialed the conference number as she perched herself up on the bar stool in her chef style kitchen to listen in. She sat at the kitchen island, her elbow resting on the spotless granite counter top. Their four sons were still asleep.

After Meesha entered the code to join the conference call, she started listening to her husband's inspiring message. She sipped on her freshly made Americano espresso, which consisted of a shot of espresso watered down with about seven ounces of hot water.

Carlton's words this morning were impactful. He had a way of making things plain and practical. He spoke about how God equips His children with everything they need to be successful in their earthly life and in the fulfillment of their dreams.

Meesha smiled as she listened intently. Her tummy felt like it was full of tiny butterflies flying around inside; Carlton had just that kind of effect on her. Hearing his voice over the phone line made her secretly blush as she thought about their lovemaking the night before.

11

Carlton was an expert lover and he didn't hold back when it came to doing whatever in order to please her. This morning, before he got out of bed, they had an encore and she was still in a state of euphoria.

"Amen. God bless you and make it a great day," she heard Carlton say as the morning call ended. Meesha shook her head slightly. She couldn't believe that she'd zoned out during Carlton's devotion. It amazed her that after twelve years of marriage she still felt like a newlywed.

She got down off the bar stool and headed upstairs to wake the boys. She went to eleven year old Carlton, Jr.'s room first because he was always the hardest to wake up. The other boys, eight-year-old Marlon, seven-year old Malik, and five-year old Micah usually woke up easily. She only had to monitor them to make sure they groomed themselves properly before coming downstairs to eat breakfast.

When they finished eating, they went to the study to speak to their father before Meesha drove them to school.

After returning home, Meesha went to the study and peeked in on Carlton. He was deep in the throes of studying his message for Sunday.

She walked over quietly to him, stood behind him as he sat at his dark walnut desk, and kissed him on the side of his face. She took in a deep breath, savoring the scent of his sexiness.

Carlton stopped writing, turned away from the computer, and focused his eyes on his wife.

"Good morning," he said as their lips met in a passionate kiss.

"Good morning," she answered, resting her bottom on the edge of the desk next to him.

"The boys get off okay?"

"Yes."

"Good. How did you enjoy this morning's devotion?"

Carlton always asked her opinion before and after he presented his messages and sermons. He valued Meesha's opinion because she was going to tell him the truth, and not just what she thought he wanted to hear. Most of the time, his messages were right on point. Occasionally, if he was overly tired, or going through some tough time due to attending so many funerals or making numerous visits to the hospital, it reflected in his message. However, one thing about Carlton was that he made sure he had a capable staff of ministers to help him manage and execute the hundreds of tasks that had to be done to successfully operate a church the size of Perfecting Your Faith Ministries. That included having ministers that were responsible for visiting the sick or officiating the numerous weddings and funerals. Carlton made certain that he performed his share as the senior pastor but it was impossible for one man, even twenty for that matter, to tend to a flock of 20,000.

"You did great, as usual," she said kissing him on his lips. "I'm proud of you."

"Thanks, baby." He grabbed hold to her waist and pulled her close while simultaneously rising from his chair. He wrapped his long toned arms around her as he smothered her mouth with his. When Carlton pulled away, for a few seconds they stared into each other's eyes like two star-crossed lovers.

"Are you ready for breakfast?"

"Yes, I am. I'm really hungry this morning."

"Anything in particular you want me to fix you?"

"Umm, what about your famous meatless scrambler?" he smiled.

"Okay, and I'll even throw in a bowl of grits and some toast."

"Awww, yes. That sounds good."

They walked out of his study hand in hand, Meesha's head resting against his shoulder. Life couldn't be any better in the Porter household.

Chapter 4

"Sometimes you try and ignore the obvious and shield yourself from the blunt truth; that some people are truly clueless as to how much they hurt you." Unknown

"Get out of here! I hate you." Peyton hollered, picking up the thousand-dollar baccarat vase from off the table and throwing it at Derek, missing his head by mere inches. "I know you don't love me. You only married me because you wanted to get your greedy paws on my money."

"Your money? Ha, are you kidding me? Something is wrong with you. You need mental help." Derek Hudson frowned, then stared at his thirty-five year old wife of thirteen years like he wanted to choke the life out of her. Instead, he shook his head, cursed underneath his breath, and stormed out of the family room.

That didn't deter Peyton. She followed him, hurling one filthy, vile obscenity after another. It was mid-day Saturday morning but she was already turned up.

"Now that you're Mr. Big CEO and president of Adverse City Bank, you think you're all of that. But, you're not worth two cents. Your bank account may be in the millions, but you're still nothing but white trailer park trash. You forget that I knew you when you were in college and living off of poor folk's noodles. I was the one who felt sorry for you and stuck by you, helped make you into the man you are today. I could have had any boy I wanted back then, but I chose you. But, you know what? I can't blame anyone but myself. I guess back then I took one too many Ecstasy pills." She laughed, then stumbled and almost fell but the wall held her up.

"You need to shut up and go lay your drunk behind down."

"Don't you talk to me like that. And I'm not drunk." Peyton weaved slowly, like she was walking a tight rope.

"Then don't you come at me with your crap," Derek yelled back.

"You act like you're so high and mighty. You wouldn't be who you are if it wasn't for my parents helping you out. It was my daddy who gave you a start and opened the door for you to make it in the banking industry."

"Your daddy didn't do a thing for me!"

"You're a liar. He did," Peyton screamed. "Not only did he help you get into banking, he's the one who connected you to the right people and told them about that App you invented and made you the wealthy scumbag you are today. You wouldn't have a dime if it wasn't for him and for me," she said, her words slurring as she pointed one finger of her sculptured nails at herself. She regained her footing and started walking up on him.

"You sound like a fool," said Derek, biting his bottom lip and shaking his head. She didn't see his clinched fist. It was like he was ready to pounce on her if she punched him, something she had done many times when she was in a drunken state like she was today.

"Mom, stop it already," her fourteen-year old son, Liam, pleaded as he walked in on her verbally attacking the man he idolized. "Please, Ma. Just go back to bed."

Peyton immediately refocused her attention from Derek to Liam. "Who the hell do you think you're talking to?"

Derek's hand went out, keeping his son from walking any farther into the room. "It's all right, son. I've got this."

"Hah, and who are you supposed to be?" Peyton asked, turning away from both of them and heading toward the bar area located just to the right of the family room. "I don't need this crap this early in the morning. Do what you want to do, just leave me alone," she told them both as she waved up her hand and disappeared.

This time, Derek was the one who followed. As she was about to go behind the custom designed bar to retrieve her favorite bottle of Vodka, he grabbed hold of her elbow. "No, you've had enough. Come on, you're going upstairs and sleep this off," he insisted.

Surprisingly, Peyton didn't protest. Sprigs of her curly blond hair were in her face, covering her blue bloodshot eyes. As Derek led her toward their bedroom, Liam appeared and stationed himself next to his inebriated mother.

Peyton looked at her son and started bawling. "I'm such a bad mother," she cried. "I'm sorry, baby." She sobbed while Derek continued leading her up the spiral staircase to the third floor of their elaborately decorated home.

"It's okay, Mom," Liam reassured her. "Just do what Dad says and get some rest."

She stopped walking and looked at her lanky, freckle faced, brown-eyed son who she described as the spitting image of his father.

"You're such a good son. I don't deserve you." Next, she looked to the other side at her husband. "Why do you keep putting up with me? Why don't you just divorce me? I'm ugly and I'm fat," she said, tears flowing down her pale-skinned face.

"You're not ugly and you're not fat," Derek told her in a calm, reassuring tone. "Now, come on. I'm going to put you to bed. You'll feel better after you take a nap."

Liam took hold of his mother's other arm as she took the last few steps to the third floor landing.

Peyton kissed her son on his cheek. "Thank you, baby."

"No problem, Mom. Get some sleep," Liam told her and then turned and went back downstairs while Derek continued escorting her to her bedroom.

Chapter 5

"One of the hardest parts of life is deciding whether to walk away or try harder." Unknown

"Look, I don't know why you've decided to bring up the past, and of all times tonight. I told you, she meant nothing to me."

"If she meant nothing to you, then why is she still calling your phone?" Avery held Ryker's phone in her hand with a vice like grip. "And you think I'm just supposed to trust you again? I can't do it, Ryker." Avery began to cry.

Avery was thirty-seven years old. She had given Ryker two beautiful little girls. Eight-year old Lexie looked just like her father with coffee bean brown skin, deep brown, doe shaped eyes and a head full of black hair that Avery kept in two braids that cascaded down the little girl's back. Six-year old Heather, people often said, looked more like Avery. Heather had features like Avery's French Canadian mother and African American father. Heather's hair looked more blondish brown in the summer months and darker in the winter months. Avery kept her hair in one long ponytail down the center of the little girl's back.

"Do you really want to do this? Because I don't think you do," Ryker stated while standing in front of the dresser in the bedroom, tying his tie.

"It's not my fault," she continued to cry. "And I won't let you make it my fault."

Ryker finished the last loop, surveyed his handiwork, and then turned around to face Avery who was sitting on the edge of their bed with one leg tucked underneath her Kim Kardashian bottom.

19

Shelia E. Bell

"You're the one who started this. It's your fault. You pushed me into the arms of another woman. Why don't you admit it," he accused as his voice escalated.

Avery covered her ears with both of her hands and shook her head from side to side. She quickly jumped up and ran toward the bathroom.

"Don't run now," Ryker told her. "You wanted to go here, so now we're here." He trailed behind Avery and was a second quicker than her, stopping her from closing the bathroom door in his face. "Let me refresh your memory since you seem to be having a bout of amnesia tonight." His arms flailed as he unleashed his verbal tirade. "You're the one who wanted to awaken your inner freak, I guess," he said, laughing mockingly. "It was you. Not me. You're the one who told me to find someone that was willing to share our bed. I did that. I did that for you, Avery. Remember?" Ryker was practically yelling by this time while Avery kept shaking her head and holding her hands over her ears. "Was it your sick way of trying to bring our stale relationship back to life? Huh, Avery?" Ryker kept talking.

Avery kept her hands over her ears as she went and sat down on the toilet and tucked her head between her knees.

"You all of a sudden got a word from Jesus," he wobbled his head in a sacrilegious gesture. His jaw flinched as he bit down on his bottom lip. "Then you started acting like you were sorry about it all. Well, I'm sorry, too. I'm sorry that I couldn't turn a whore into a housewife. I'm sorry I had the unmitigated gall to believe that you got with me because you loved me and not because of my fat bank account. You know what? I don't care what you think anymore. You run up to that church practically every Sunday, you and your *girls* pretending

20

like you have it all together. Who do you think you're fooling? Who, Avery?"

Ryker turned around swiftly and walked out of the bathroom. Before he left the bedroom, he walked back and stood at the bathroom door. "If you want to know why Olivia still calls me, why don't you ask her. You *should* be able to ask your own cousin," he said then stormed out of the room.

Avery got up from the toilet only to collapse onto the heated concrete tiled floor. In a balled up heap, she sobbed. She didn't know why she told Ryker she wanted to have a ménage a trois. Maybe it was because somewhere during the ten years they'd been together, their relationship seemed to have hit a brick wall.

Ryker had faired quite well as a prominent, well-respected attorney, so much so that he was a millionaire several times over. When Avery met him, he was in Las Vegas attending one of the largest trial attorney conventions in the country. She, along with several more ladies, had been set up to provide special entertainment. Ryker and some other attorneys were treated to a private set complete with strippers who weren't afraid to take it all off and give the gentlemen whatever they asked for, as long as the money was right. Avery was one of those girls.

When Ryker asked her for a private dance in his hotel suite, for the right price, she obliged him. She usually didn't get involved with her clients, but something about Ryker was different. He was a fairly decent looking man, but Avery had seen better, lots better. He was average height, about five nine, had a slight gut on him from eating what she figured was plenty of steak. She remembered that he had the most gorgeous smile she'd seen a man display, and his teeth had to have been braced when he was younger because they were perfectly

21

Shelia E. Bell

straight and white as snow. He was kind to her that evening and she broke another one of her cardinal rules, which was not to fall for her customers. That night, not only did she sleep with Ryker, she spent the night with him, and the next night and the next night, and every night after that up until the time he had to leave Las Vegas and return to Florida.

She didn't see him again after that until about seven months later. As fate would have it, she moved to Florida with her aunt and her family because she wanted a new start and a chance to start her life fresh.

Avery had been in Florida for less than two months when she saw Ryker walking into a restaurant where she had gotten a job as a server. When she saw him, he was accompanied by three other men. All of them looking good, real good in their black suits, white shirts, and designer ties and shoes. She was lucky enough to be the waitress for their table that day. At first, she was nervous to go to his table, not sure what he was going to say, or if he would even remember her. But her apprehension quickly faded when he watched her as she took their orders. After she memorized all of their orders, Ryker smiled and winked at her.

At the end of her shift that evening, he returned to the restaurant and asked her to go out with him. She couldn't believe that he would want to see her again. To make sure he understood that she had turned over a new leaf in her life, she let him know right away that the girl he met in Las Vegas was not the woman he was talking to today.

Ryker seemed pleased. He asked her if she would consider going out on a real date with him that weekend coming up. She accepted and they had been an item ever since.

Now, here it was, nine years later, and he still hadn't legally made her his wife, but no one knew that. Not

22

Peyton. Not Eva. Not Meesha. No one. She'd given him children, and he'd given her the 8,600 square foot, three story house, they lived in and anything his money could buy. She tried to be a good wife and mother, but she felt like a phony. Maybe that's why she did what she did. Maybe she wanted to see if he would really go for having a threesome, when deep down inside she didn't want him to agree to do it. She was confused, had been drinking that night, and once it came out, there was no turning back because after Ryker got over the initial shock of what she suggested, he acted like he was all for it.

She pulled herself up slowly from the bathroom floor, got dressed and silently thanked God that Lexie and Heather were spending the weekend with Ryker's parents. The house was empty. The housekeeper wouldn't be back until tomorrow morning and only God knew when Ryker would return. She had plenty of time to kill herself.

Chapter 6

"Only your real friends will tell you when your face is dirty." Sicilian Proverb

Dressed to the hilt in their church attire, Eva Stenberg minus Harper, and Peyton with Derek and Liam strolled into Perfecting Your Faith Ministries. The sanctuary was filling up quickly as it did every Sunday morning. They held three services; 8 a.m., 10 a.m., and 11:45 a.m. The housewives attended the ten o'clock service most of the time. On occasion, they would attend the first service so they could get their church time done and out of the way.

The four of them made their way to the middle of the sanctuary toward their seats. It wasn't like they owned special seats in the mega church, but it was like an unspoken word that they all sat in the same section and on the same rows every Sunday.

When they made it to their seats, Derek and Liam stood to the side, allowing Eva and Peyton to sit down first before Liam took the seat closest to his mother. Derek sat next to his son.

"Have you talked to Avery?" Peyton asked Eva, turning slightly around to face her as they walked down the carpeted aisle to their seats.

"No, I called her a couple of times last night, but she didn't answer her phone."

"I texted her last night, but she didn't answer me either. I hope she and Ryker haven't gotten into another one of their spats. You know how that goes," Peyton said, talking softly so Derek and Liam wouldn't hear her. She didn't want to hear Derek telling her that she talked too much, which he often did.

24

Eva and Peyton continued to talk until Meesha appeared and halted the conversation.

"Good morning, Derek. Hello, Liam." Looking past Derek and over at Liam sitting next to him, she smiled. "Young man, I think you get more handsome every time I see you," she complimented. Liam blushed and his complexion turned blood red.

"Thank you, Mrs. Porter," Liam said most politely.

"How are *you*, Meesha?" asked Derek.

"I'm blessed. I have absolutely nothing to complain about." Fashionably dressed in a Dolce & Gabbana russet brown raw silk pants suit, Meesha laid her butter soft hand on top of his hand and squeezed it affectionately but not in a disrespectful manner. She leaned in, excusing herself, and extended her diamond-encrusted hand out toward Peyton and repeated the gesture.

Eva lifted her hand up for Meesha to shake it as well. "Good morning, my sisters in Christ," Meesha said.

Peyton rolled her eyes up in her head. "Good morning." Peyton released a fake smile, slightly shaking her head. She never got over how differently Meesha talked and acted when she was at church versus when she was hanging out with them. She sounded so... well... like she was flodging. Anyway, Peyton was used to it so she went along with the program just as she did every Sunday.

"I'm okay," Eva responded, her voice dragging.

Neither Meesha nor Peyton had to ask Eva what was wrong with her and why she was sounding so dry. They knew it was probably because once again, Harper was absent.

"Where's Avery?" Meesha asked, eyeing Peyton and Eva questioningly.

Eva shrugged and Peyton's eyebrows lifted.

"Haven't talked to her since early yesterday," Eva replied.

"Neither have I," Peyton said.

"I haven't either," Meesha added. The musicians started playing as the curtains rose slowly, revealing the 500-member choir. "Have to go." Meesha hurriedly stepped back, threw her hand up at her friends. "We'll talk this afternoon." She turned and walked toward the front of the sanctuary to her reserved seat.

After the choir sang a couple of songs, Carlton got up from his seat in the pulpit and approached the podium.

"Good morning, Perfecting Your Faith. It's good to be in the house of the Lord isn't it?" He stood erect, shoulders back, not too tall but definitely not too short. His neatly trimmed salt and pepper, short, boxed beard, coupled with his milk chocolate skin seemed to enhance his navy designer sharkskin suit that was perfectly tailored to his physique. His mild mannered voice had a captivating presence as he addressed his congregation.

"It's a blessing to be here this morning. It makes me feel good when I can come here Sunday after Sunday and look out and see what God is doing."

The congregation could be heard saying, *Amen* and *Praise God* as Carlton continued.

"This morning, I want to take a few minutes to talk to you about heart trouble. If you have your Bibles, *and* you should, turn with me to Jeremiah chapter seventeen and verse nine. Reading from the Living Bible it says, "The heart is the most deceitful thing there is and desperately wicked. No one can really know how bad it is!""

Carlton preached with zeal for the next thirty minutes. By the time he ended his sermon, the congregation could be seen and heard shouting *hallelujah, praise God.* People poured down to the front of the church to be prayed for. Others came to commit their lives to Christ or become members of Perfecting Your Faith. Pastor Carlton wiped the sweat from his brow as he stood in the midst of the crowd praying and giving God his own personal thanks.

Meesha, not shy at all, and totally in support of her husband, joined him and the ministers and elders in praying and addressing the needs of the people.

Eva leaned over and whispered to Peyton, "I'm out. I'll talk to you later." She grabbed her oversized handbag and started to stand, but Peyton stopped her by grabbing hold of her arm.

"Is everything okay?"

"Yeah, I just want to beat the crowd. You know how long it takes to get off this parking lot." Eva looked around the sanctuary and back at Peyton. "You see all the people leaving already. Church is over," she whispered.

"Yeah, but you know how much Carlton dislikes it when people leave before he gives his blessing. It's not going to take long for them to finish up. You know he has to get ready for the eleven forty-five service." This time Peyton looked away from Eva and focused her eyes on the people being ministered to. Some of them had already been prayed for and had already turned to go back to their seats. "See, they're almost done."

Eva shrugged, sighed, and relaxed back against the pew. She decided that she would text Avery to see if she would get a response.

"Why aren't u at church? Everything ok?"

No response.

When church ended, it didn't take long for Eva to get off the church parking lot considering the endless number of cars coming and going. The parking lot attendants were good at keeping down traffic congestion on the huge parking area. She turned right out of the parking lot, heading toward Lincoln Drive when her cell phone rang.

Avery's name appeared. Eva pushed the button on her steering wheel to answer the call.

"It's Ryker. Are you at church?" He sounded upset.

"I'm just leaving. What's going on? Where is Avery? I've been trying to reach her since yesterday."

"She's in the hospital."

"Hospital? Why? What happened?" Eva asked, trying not to panic.

"She..." he went silent.

"She what? You're scaring me, Ryker. What happened to Avery?" This time she didn't try to hold back the fear in her voice. Something had to be drastically wrong for Ryker to call her. Out of the four housewives, Eva and Avery were especially close, but that didn't make Ryker didn't care too much for her. For some reason, unbeknownst to Eva, he was not too fond of her. Eva didn't know if it was because of her ethnicity or if it was because he probably knew that Avery told her just about everything that went on between them. As of now, she didn't have time to figure it out; something was wrong with Avery and she needed to know what it was.

"Tell me what's wrong," she almost yelled into the phone.

"Eva tried to kill herself. She's at Adverse General."

Eva's hand flew up to her mouth while she kept the other one pinned to the steering wheel. She altered her direction and instead of going toward her home on Lincoln Drive, she took the first left turn she could make and headed in the direction of Adverse General.

"Oh, my God," she cried. "Kill herself? When? How? Is...is she...de—"

"No, she's not dead, but she's not out of the woods either."

"When did this happen?"

"Sometime last night. Looks like she took an overdose of those pain pills the doctor prescribed after she was in that car wreck a few months ago. Thank God, I came home when I did. I got home earlier than I expected. That's when I found her on the floor of our bathroom."

Terror resonated in his voice. Peyton could tell that he was truly distraught.

"I'm on my way," Eva said, ending the call. She immediately called Peyton to tell her the tragic news.

Why would Avery do such a thing? The more Eva thought about it, the angrier she became. She already summed up that it had to have had something to do with Ryker. Had he been cheating on Avery again? Was he threatening to leave her and take the kids like he'd done before? Whatever the reason, Eva tried hard not to concentrate on it. Her main objective was to get to the hospital. She wanted to see for herself if Avery was going to be all right.

Chapter 7

"True friends stab you in the front." Oscar Wilde

The following evening, Pastor Porter and the housewives gathered in Avery's hospital room. Though she was improving physically after having her stomach pumped, her mental state was still in shambles. The psychiatrist talked about moving her to the mental health floor of Adverse General.

"I don't know what you could have been thinking?" voiced Eva. "Nothing is worth killing yourself over."

Avery turned her head toward the window and away from her friends. She felt ashamed and embarrassed. The thought of leaving her daughters, leaving her family and friends, was almost too much to bear. But it wasn't all her fault. She refused to take the full blame for her actions. It was Ryker's fault too. He had managed to make her feel like she was worthless. The fact that she had changed her life when she fell in love with him didn't seem to count for anything because he still felt that it was okay for her to be cheated on and walked on by him. She felt like she was unworthy, but she never would have thought that she, of all people, would try to end her own life. Yet, lying in the hospital bed with Pastor Porter, Meesha, Peyton, and Eva staring at her like she was an animal in a zoo was a harsh reminder that that's exactly what she'd attempted to do.

"I wish you would have come to me. I would have helped you to make it through whatever it was you felt like you couldn't face any longer," Meesha said, her voice sounding sad for her friend.

"If I can survive through my messed up life and marriage, I know you should be able to," Peyton told

30

Avery. "Do you think it's easy living with a man who practically despises me? He calls me names, he finds every excuse to stay away from home, and he definitely won't make love to me."

Carlton flinched as he listened to Peyton, clearly feeling like he was being made privy to too much information.

"All you had to deal with was Ryker cheating on you." Peyton raised up one shaky finger. "One, not multiple, just one affair, and you're ready to take yourself out."

"You don't know what you're talking about," Avery said, her voice full of anger and hurt. "You think it's easy for me to deal with his infidelity? Well, I'm not you, Peyton. I don't drown my worries in a bottle of Vodka."

"You're right, you drown your worries in a bottle of pills," Peyton snapped back. "And look where it's gotten you."

"Stop it, ladies," Carlton Porter insisted. "This is not what friends do to support each other. They build each other up, not tear one another down."

"Yeah, Carlton is right. Stop all of this bickering. It's not going to solve anything," said Eva.

"Look, Avery, we're here because we care about you," Meesha explained. "And we're glad you're going to be all right. If you have to spend a few days in a mental health facility, or here at Adverse General, then so be it. As long as you're able to get some professional help and counseling."

Avery cried as Carlton came close to the side of her bed and took hold of her hand. He stroked her matted hair and pushed back several stray strands from off her forehead. In a compassionate and loving tone, he leaned down close to Avery. "God loves you, Avery. He cares about what you're going through.

Shelia E. Bell

"Do you care, too, Pastor? Do you love me too?" Avery cried.

Clearing his throat, he answered, "We all love you, Avery."

Meesha walked up next to him as Carlton continued to gently massage Avery's hand. "Everything is going to be just fine. You just wait and see. Until then, know that we're here for you," she said, looking over her shoulder at Eva and Peyton.

"She's right," Eva said, standing on the other side of Meesha.

Carlton released Avery's hand, kissed her lightly on her forehead, and stepped away. "I'm going to let you get some rest now. I'll be back to check on you and pray with you tomorrow," Carlton said. "But if you need me before then, please just call me or Meesha."

Avery looked at Carlton with tears crested in her eyes and responded by turning her head away.

Carlton left the hospital while Meesha remained. When he was told that Avery had tried to commit suicide, he had been conducting the ministerial staff Bible Study. He ordered one of the other ministers to take over while one of his drivers rushed him to Adverse General to see how she was. Carlton understood that Avery had gone through a lot in her marriage and was quite vulnerable. He couldn't see himself not going to be by her side. It was his job and his pastoral duty.

"I still want to know why you downed a bottle of pills. What was so terribly wrong?" Peyton pressured after Carlton left.

"I didn't tell you the whole story about me and Ryker. I didn't tell you that I was the one who drove him into the arms of another woman."

"What are you talking about?" asked Eva. "How are you responsible for Ryker going outside of his marriage?

32

I won't let you take the blame for something that's totally his fault."

"Yeah, he made that choice," said Meesha.

"Listen to me," Avery insisted. "When Ryker and I first met, I was a stripper, a high priced call girl, a whore."

Meesha, Eva, and Peyton stared. Peyton's mouth dropped open and Eva's eyes bucked, while Meesha shook her head, placing one hand over her mouth to shield her surprise.

"That's not all. I was the one that suggested that Ryker and me have a threesome. I wanted to give him something special, something unique for his birthday."

"Something special and unique? Couldn't you have taken the man to the Super Bowl or something?" mocked Peyton.

Meesha turned slightly and gave Peyton a dirty look.

"I'm just saying," Peyton responded. "How did she think that bringing someone else into their bed would make him love her more? Tell me, Avery, was it a man or a woman?"

Avery looked like she was about to cry. "It was Olivia."

"Olivia? Your cousin Olivia?" repeated Eva. "The attorney Olivia?"

Avery nodded as tears rolled down her cheeks.

"You were a whore and your husband's mistress is your cousin?" said Peyton and chuckled. "Wow, what else is there that we don't know about you. I need to be taking notes so I can put it in a novel."

Meesha held up her hand in a motion for Peyton to stop talking. "Look, you need to get some rest. Now is not the time to talk about all of this. Eva...Peyton, it's time for us to leave."

"Speak for yourself," Peyton said. "I'm not quite ready to leave, and apparently Avery feels like she needs to get this off her chest. Right, Avery?" Peyton looked down at Avery.

"Meesha's right. I'm tired. I want to be alone. Thank you for coming."

"You two go on," Eva told Meesha and Peyton. "I'm going to sit here a while longer."

"No need, Eva. I want to rest. I hope you understand." Avery said.

"Of course, I understand. I'll call and check on you later."

"Okay, buh-bye," Avery said to her friends.

"Avery, I hope you feel better. Take care of yourself so you can hurry up and get out of this God-awful place. Our ladies day out is coming up, and I refuse to be left with these two." Peyton walked over, leaned down, and kissed Avery on her cheek. "I'll call and check on you later," she said, sounding sincere.

"Okay," Avery replied.

"Can I pray for you before we leave?" Meesha asked.

Avery slowly nodded.

Meesha extended her hands on each side of her. The women held hands and Meesha began to pray for her friend.

■

"Can you believe Avery was a prostitute? I'm absolutely stunned," Peyton said as Eva drove to their neighborhood.

Eva shook her head. "I know, right. I can't believe it either. But still, that shouldn't have caused her to want to kill herself. I'm just saying."

Peyton continued her comments. "People take themselves out for far less. And on top of that, her cousin is screwing Ryker? This is some made for TV kind of drama."

Eva turned on the street leading to their neighborhood. "I don't know what to say." Eva shook her head and upturned her mouth. "You never know about people."

"Nope, you sure don't. Maybe seeing a psychiatrist, someone who can help her deal with her past mistakes, will be good for her," said Peyton, sounding compassionate for the first time.

Eva drove along the winding, private, black-topped road leading to Peyton's house. She pulled up in front of the front steps and stopped, but didn't turn off the car. "I'll talk to you later."

"Sure. Thanks. I'm going to go in here, kick off my shoes, make me a good stiff nightcap, and chill. This has been one exciting day. I deserve it." She opened the car door, got out and before she closed the door, she looked in the driver's window at Eva. "If this gets out in the tabloids, they're going to have a field day."

"That's why we have to keep this between the four of us. No one else can know."

"Yeah, I know. Anyway, see you later." Peyton swished off without waiting on a response.

Chapter 8

"The oldest and strongest emotion of mankind is fear, and the oldest and strongest kind of fear is fear of the unknown." H. P. Lovecraft

Peyton was in the sitting room of their master bedroom nursing her third shot of Vodka, and thinking about the mess Avery had made of her life. She could understand how the past could damage the future to a point where, like Avery, you might feel hopeless. It didn't matter how much she believed in God. The fact that Avery's past wouldn't let go of her, was the problem, and Peyton felt her friend's pain.

Peyton stumbled, got up from the sofa, and made her way over to the luxury hotel-like refrigerated vanity inside the room. She opened its door and removed a chilled bottle of Vodka and with shaking hands, she tried pouring another shot into her glass. The glass slid from her hand, landing on the well-kept, high finished dark hardwoods. Rather than pick up the glass, Peyton opened the bottle of Vodka, put it up to her mouth and took a large gulp before putting the top back on it, placing it in the vanity and returning back to the sofa.

Her eyes swelled with tears as she thought about the haunting secrets of her own past. There were nights when she woke up in a sweat, terrified that Derek or God forbid, her friends and family, would discover the dark secret she herself was hiding.

She never intended to do anything to break the law, but she had to save him. She couldn't stand back and watch him being abused. He was just a child. A little boy with no one to care about him.

The day it happened, Peyton knew that God was on her side. The little boy had been left at home all alone;

36

and it just happened to be the day before she was scheduled to return to Chicago, where she'd established a comfortable life.

For the past two months, she had been in Memphis after moving there because of Winston, a wonderful man she had met online. After communicating back and forth for almost a year, she accepted his offer to come and visit him for a couple of weeks. Winston had come to see her in Chicago a few times during their long distance relationship, so they both had hopes that their relationship could work. Unfortunately, things didn't turn out that way after she made the trip to Memphis. He was a really nice guy, but he did not satisfy her at all. They both finally concluded that there was no real love connection.

As a sales and marketing executive for a national pharmaceutical company, Peyton was blessed to be in a position to work from just about any location outside her company's headquarters in Chicago. She hung around Memphis, enjoying the city and working from a loft apartment she short term leased in downtown Memphis.

While in Memphis, Peyton reached out on Facebook and found one of her old college friends named Breyonna. She thought it would be nice to see Breyonna after all this time, plus it would hopefully give her someone to hang out with while she was in Memphis.

It took a couple of weeks before Peyton heard back from Breyonna, but she was excited to learn that Breyonna still lived in the city. The two former friends decided to meet for lunch downtown. When Peyton met up with her, she immediately saw that Breyonna hadn't fared as well as she had when she was in college. In fact, Breyonna's life was troubled and harsh. Breyonna confessed that she was a heroin addict.

Peyton helped Breyonna by buying her a few items of clothing, giving her money for food, and she even paid

Breyonna's rent when she learned that she was about to be evicted. Breyonna started calling Peyton. Sometimes they talked like normal. A couple of times, she met up with Breyonna and they went out to eat. Breyonna ate like a rabbit. She would much rather have drugs.

Peyton grew somewhat concerned when she received a phone call from her late one evening. Breyonna told her she was in trouble and she needed her help. The phone went dead while Breyonna was talking. Peyton tried to call her back but the phone went to voicemail. She tried several more times, and the same thing happened. The following day, Peyton tried calling Breyonna again, but she still couldn't get in touch with her. This time when she called her, the number she'd given Peyton was disconnected, and when Peyton went on Facebook to try to track her down, Breyonna's page was deactivated. Peyton grew worried because usually, every few days, Breyonna would call and ask her for a few dollars. Peyton was no fool; she knew that Breyonna was more than likely using the money to buy drugs, but Peyton had a soft spot for the girl, especially after Breyonna told her that she had a little boy.

Peyton decided that she would go check on Breyonna at her apartment which was located in a gang and drug infested neighborhood. Peyton had been there twice before, but had never gone inside. She hoped Breyonna and her son were okay. She'd heard too many horror stories about drug addicted mothers and their kids, and she hoped Breyonna hadn't become a statistic.

Peyton thought about the last time she saw Breyonna. Breyonna had her son with her. He looked dirty, hungry, and frightened. Peyton took the both of them to get something to eat. She even bought the little boy a toy. Before she dropped them off at her apartment, Peyton strongly cautioned Breyonna to take better care of her child before the authorities stepped in and took him away.

When she arrived unannounced that morning, Peyton knocked on the door to the apartment. No one answered. She knocked several more times. She was about to leave when she heard a childlike cry coming from the other side of the apartment door. She knocked on the door again. Still, no answer. Peyton, frightened and nervous, turned the doorknob, and much to her surprise, it was unlocked. She called Breyonna's name as she slowly opened the door. The stench filled her nostrils as she called Breyonna's name again, making another step into the apartment. It was filthy. Trash was everywhere.

Peyton walked deeper into the apartment. She was stunned when she saw the little boy huddled on the side of the bed, crying. Peyton picked him up gingerly. His hands and arms were riddled with bruises. She had to call the police, someone to come and get the child. Just as she was about to contact the authorities, Breyonna appeared. From the look on her face, Peyton could tell that she was high.

"What are you doing with my kid?" Breyonna charged at Peyton. "Give me my kid," she said followed by a long stream of expletives as she reached out to take the toddler away from Peyton.

"What is wrong with you? Why would you leave him alone? You're a mother. You need to stop messing with those drugs and get yourself some help."

"I don't need help. Plus, my li'l sister been watching him. This is my business anyway," Breyonna lashed out.

Peyton's hand flew up to her mouth. "What is wrong with you?"

"I don't have to explain anything to you." Breyonna's words were slurred.

"You're pathetic."

Breyonna laughed and stumbled forward. She almost dropped the little boy from her arms, but Peyton grabbed him just in time.

"You think you can do a better job? You want him? Then gimme a grand and he's yours."

"What? Are you serious?" Peyton looked at the little boy and then she looked at Breyonna. "You're crazy."

"I would think you would want him. After all, he *is* Carlton Porter's kid. You still love you some Carlton, I bet." Breyonna teased and laughed, while struggling to maintain her balance. Her eyes looked like she could hardly see.

"Girl, you sound crazy and stupid! You're more than high, you're delusional."

"Oh, it's his kid alright and that's fa sho. And you don't know everything about Carlton's business. I bet you didn't know that me and him hook up and get our high on together every time he comes through Memphis for one of those church conventions he attends."

"I don't believe that!" Peyton shouted, holding the boy tighter. "You are such a liar. You always have been."

"I don't have to prove anything to you, so I definitely don't have to lie. I bet a lot of people would be shocked at the double life that man leads. Pretending like he's so into God and all, but he hunts me down every time he sets foot in this city. He can't get enough of this." Breyonna pointed at herself like she was a beauty queen. She used to be a beautiful girl but drugs had aged her considerably. "He loves to get high, too. So I give him everything he wants when he's here. And this is what he left me with the last time he hit this city." She looked at the little boy with disgust who appeared to be a little over one but not quite two years old.

Peyton was absolutely appalled at all the things Breyonna told her.

"Anyway, this kid ain't nothing but trouble. He's holding me back. The next time he came here, I was going to tell Carlton that he knocked me up, but now that you've come along...anyway, what you wanna do? You want him or not?"

Peyton didn't think a second too long. She drove to the bank with Breyonna and the little boy, withdrew the money, and gave it to her in exchange for the little boy - that was the day Peyton became a mother.

That happened twelve years ago, and she hadn't heard anything from Breyonna since. Through the years, Peyton searched online and on social media, but she couldn't find anything about her. She started to hire a private investigator but decided against it. She felt it was best to let sleeping dogs lie. As far as the boy being Carlton Porter's kid, Peyton believed Breyonna told her that to toy around with her because she knew that Peyton used to be in love with Carlton. Their relationship didn't work out because back then Carlton had a strong penchant for messing around with lots of girls and drugs.

After graduating from ACU, with the help of his father, Carlton secured a high-level position at a medical device company in Adverse City. He began to carve a highly successful life and career for himself but the call to ministry was something he could not seem to shake, so he returned to school and studied theology. Fresh out of divinity school, Carlton met and later married Meesha. He founded Perfecting Your Faith shortly thereafter. All Meesha ever knew was that Peyton and Carlton knew each other from when they both attended ACU.

Peyton returned to Chicago with the little boy that she told everyone she had adopted. She later met Derek, fell in love, got married, and moved to Florida. With each day that passed, Peyton convinced herself over the years that it was God who had allowed her to find love, unconditional love, in a little unwanted boy she named Liam.

Chapter 9

"I wish you told me from the start that you were gonna break my heart." Unknown

The housewives gathered at Zodiac Café at Neiman Marcus, one of their favorite places to meet. It was located inside Bal Harbour Shops, an upscale, open-air shopping mall they frequented. This was the first ladies' day out they'd had since Avery was discharged from the hospital three weeks ago.

They studied their menus while they talked and caught up on what had been going on in each of their lives.

"Meesha, you're awfully quiet. What's on your mind?" Eva asked, looking up from her menu.

Peyton stared and so did Avery.

"Why are you all staring at me?"

"Like Eva said, you're sitting over there all quiet. Something's on your mind," Peyton spoke up.

"She's trying to decide what she's going to eat," Avery replied.

"Avery's right. I'm trying to decide what I'm having today."

"Girl, we've been to this place a hundred times, and you order the same thing every time. You know the menu like you know the back of your hand, so don't play. Now, tell us what's going on," Peyton insisted.

Meesha laid the menu down on the table, pursed her lips, and looked at each one of her friends like she was trying to decide if she could trust them. She finally released an audible sigh, closed and opened her eyes and then spoke.

"Carlton wants a divorce."

Eva's hand flew up to her mouth. Peyton picked up her glass and took a big swallow of her cosmopolitan.

Avery immediately spoke. "You can't be serious. Please tell us this is some kind of joke."

"I wish I could tell you that I was joking, but I can't." Her eyes teared up.

The waitress came to take their orders so the housewives put their conversation on pause, placed their orders, and waited for the waitress to turn and leave.

"But why?" Avery inquired.

"Yeah, why?" asked Eva. "You and Carlton are the perfect couple. I've never even heard that man say one cross word to you."

"Well, nothing surprises me these days. I don't care how perfect things look on the outside."

Eva rolled her eyes at Peyton. "Do you have a sympathetic bone in your body?" she recoiled.

"I'm just telling you what God loves—the truth."

"When did he tell you?" Eva turned from Peyton and looked at Meesha who was wiping a tear from her face with the ball of her finger.

"A few days ago," Meesha explained, looking briefly at Eva. "He said he couldn't do it anymore. Said he wasn't happy and that he hadn't been happy for a long time. He swore that it wasn't another woman, but he had been praying about it for a long time, and he felt finally that God had released him to tell me how he felt." More tears came.

"That's a bunch of crap," Peyton retorted. "There's no way a man, especially a man like Carlton Porter, is going to tell you he wants a divorce because he isn't happy. There has to be a woman, or, God forbid, I hope it isn't a man in his life."

"You're too much," Avery said. "A man? Why are your thoughts so perverted?"

"That's not perverted; that's just real talk. You, of all people, should know how freaky people can be," Peyton bit back.

"You know what, Peyton, I don't see why Derek stays with you. You're nothing but a drunk and a hater. No wonder he's disgusted by you," Avery snapped.

Peyton rolled her eyes at Avery, hurriedly picked up her glass, and took the last swallow of her drink. "Excuse me," she said to their waitress when she saw her waiting on one of the customers nearby. "Bring me a vodka on the rocks."

"Drinking yourself to death is not going to make your problems go away," Avery told her.

"Neither is choking down a bottle full of Percocet," Peyton replied with a tinge of venom in her voice. "But you did it. Now what?" she retorted angrily.

"Stop it, both of you," Eva scolded under her breath. "This is not the time or the place. Meesha," Eva said. "If you don't want to talk about it, you don't have to."

"He said he felt like a hypocrite standing in the pulpit Sunday after Sunday knowing that he didn't feel the way he once felt about me. He said he wanted the divorce to be quiet and that he would give me the house, and make sure me and the kids were financially taken care of. He even went so far as to say that he had already spoken to an attorney that guess who recommended?" Meesha eyed Avery.

"Ryker?" said Eva.

"Ryker?" repeated Avery. "I swear I didn't know. He hasn't said a word to me."

"Well, your husband referred him to a divorce lawyer, one of the best from what I've heard. But it's all good. I can't fault Ryker or anyone else for Carlton's actions."

"That insensitive dog," mouthed Peyton.

The waitress interrupted their conversation once more, placing their orders on the table.

The ladies toyed around with their food and for several moments they sat at the table engaged in silence.

"I don't know what I'm going to do," Meesha said, breaking the silence, as she used her fork to stir around in her vegetable fruit salad. "He hasn't said anything about moving out. It's like he told me all of this in one day, and he hasn't said anything since."

Eva used her fork to slice off a piece of her blackened salmon and put it in her mouth. "I don't know what to say. I do know that if I were you, I would not let him have custody of my children."

"You don't know what you would do, Eva. You don't have children, so don't be so quick to shell out parental advice," Peyton warned.

Eva looked hurt by Peyton's remarks. "You can be so cruel when you drink," Eva told her.

"What I said has nothing to do with drinking. It's the truth. You shouldn't do that."

Avery spoke up and turned her attention to Meesha. "We're here for you. Just let us know what you need." Avery looked at Peyton and Eva before returning her gaze toward Meesha.

Meesha opened her bag and brought out some tissue. She wiped her tears a final time before saying, "God is not going to let this happen. Carlton is going to realize that he loves me and that we're supposed to be together until death do us part. Everything is going to work out. It has to."

Peyton, who minutes earlier had been condescending, reached across the table, taking hold of Meesha's hand. "You're right. Everything is going to work out just fine. You'll see. Don't you worry about a thing."

After they finished eating, the women convinced Meesha to join them on a shopping excursion. At first Meesha balked against the idea. All she wanted to do was go home, and crawl up in her bed.

"Look, you know what I just went through, Meesha. It's only by the grace of God that I'm still alive. I don't want you to sink into a deep hole of depression like I did. I'm still trying to recover. But, slowly I'm beginning to understand that no matter how bad things get, it's not worth giving up on life and living." Avery stood in front of Meesha as the women surrounded her outside in the restaurant parking lot.

"Avery's right. I know it hurts. I can't even begin to imagine your pain, but you have a strong belief system," Eva reminded her. "You're always telling us to seek God, to have faith, and to never give up. Well, we're here to remind you that you have to do the same. You can't throw in the towel. You can't allow Carlton to make you give up on your faith."

"God is in control. Isn't that what you always say?" said Peyton.

Meesha wiped more tears from her face. Eva stepped closer to her as Avery moved slightly to the side. Eva wrapped her arms around her friend. Avery and Peyton joined in and the three of them held on to Meesha as if they were trying desperately to save her life.

As they stepped back, Meesha looked at her friends. "Okay, I'll go, but I have to be back in time to pick up the boys."

"You'll be back in time," Eva assured her.

"You all can leave your cars here, and ride with me," Avery offered.

"No, that's okay. I'll drive my own car," said Meesha. "I'll be fine."

"Peyton, you already know that we are not going to let you drive, so what's it going to be? Who are you riding with?" asked Eva.

"I'll ride with Meesha since you have Avery with you. I'll come back and get my car later, or I'll get someone to get it for me."

"Come on. My car is right over there," Meesha said, pointing to the right of her.

"We'll meet you there," Eva said as she and Avery turned away from Meesha and Peyton and walked the few steps to Eva's car.

While shopping, Peyton indulged in a highly overpriced blouse while Eva purchased an equally pricey handbag to add to her already extensive collection. By the time they did their retail damage, the ladies left the mall happy and smiling, at least on the outside.

Chapter 10

"Love is not about how long you can wait for someone, but about how well you understand why it is you're waiting. Unknown*

Eva dropped Avery off at home and headed to her house, prepared to spend another evening alone in a huge empty space that was supposed to be home. On the drive, she turned up the radio and listened to Bruno Mars singing. *"…I should've bought you flowers and held your hand. Should've gave you all my hours when I had the chance…"*

Once inside, she carried out her usual routine. She lit scented candles around the Jacuzzi tub that was big enough for four people, but one that she always shared alone. When they first moved into what she thought would be her dream house, it was this bathroom, and the luxurious Jacuzzi tub that Eva fell hard for. She imagined her and Harper making love in that tub, and afterward she would lay her back against his naked chest as the warmth of the water kissed their skin, denoting satisfaction.

Her dreams quickly disintegrated when Harper was appointed Medical Director and Adverse General's Chief Cardiologist. He practically resided at Adverse General Hospital, leaving her feeling desperately alone and unloved.

"Harper?" she called out as she soaked in the tub. "Is that you?" she asked when she heard what sounded like someone moving around in the bedroom.

There was no answer. Eva's heart picked up its pace as she eased up and sat upright in the tub. How could someone have broken in? The alarm would have sounded. Maybe they'd found a way to disarm it. She became terrified as she heard a shuffling sound. Her breath quickened as the shuffling changed into footsteps. She watched as the handle turned ever so slowly on the closed bathroom door. *God, please help me.* She looked over her right shoulder for the alarm button on the back wall of the tub. She reached her hand to push it when the door swung open.

With one hand over her chest, she sighed heavily. "My God, Harper. Why didn't you say something?" she asked as he slowly entered the bathroom.

"I thought this would say it all," he replied as he walked over to the tub in nothing but his birthday suit.

Eva studied her husband's chiseled physique. His skin was flawless. His muscled calves, long legs, and perfect six-pack made her so weak that she felt like she would faint at the sexiness that exuded from him.

Harper sauntered over to the tub, looking down at his wife for several seconds before he stepped inside the tub. He sat down on the other end, and gently pulled her close, cutting off her breath with kisses. What he did next made Eva forget about all the hours, days, and weeks that he had left her all alone, and without hesitation she completely yielded her body to his.

After their lovemaking, he helped her out of the tub, dried her off, and led her to their bed.

Quietly, Eva lay spent inside the crook of Harper's arm. She kissed his chest lightly before looking up at him.

Harper's eyes were closed, but when he tightened his arm around her shoulder, she knew he wasn't asleep.

"I want a baby," she said timidly.

She immediately felt Harper's grip loosen and his body tensed up. "We've been married almost three years. Why can't we have a baby?"

Harper released her, sat up on the side of the bed, and then stood up.

"Where are you going?" Eva sat up in the bed. "I asked you one simple question and you have to get up like you're upset with me?"

Harper turned around and looked down at his wife. "Why did you have to ruin a perfect evening with talk about having a baby? You know how I feel about that. All of the hours I spend away from home. It wouldn't be fair to bring a kid into a house that will primarily be up to one parent, which is you, to raise."

"Harper, everything will be fine. You won't always be away at the hospital. And I promise, I'll be a good mother."

"You being a good mother has nothing to do with it and you know it. We've had this conversation too many times before, and like I always tell you, this is not the right time to bring a kid into the world."

Harper turned from Eva and walked toward the bathroom.

Eva got up from the bed, removed her robe from the side chair nearby, put it on, and followed him.

"Then tell me when is the time going to be right, Harper? I'm tired of your excuses."

Harper stopped and looked over his shoulder at her. "I had my son when I was in the throes of establishing my medical career. I knew nothing about being a father, and at the time, I didn't want to learn, so consequently I was horrible at it. I lost out on being a real father. I didn't see him take his first step, or say his first words. Nothing. I was too wrapped up in becoming successful so I could provide the finer things of life to him. But I looked up one day and it was too late."

"But why are you blaming me? I shouldn't be made to suffer because his mother left you and married someone else."

"It's more to it than her marrying someone else; another man raised my son. Now, he's a twenty-three year old man, and we barely know each other."

"I don't agree. You and Seth have a good relationship."

"Really?" Harper smirked. "Are you serious? When was the last time he came to Adverse City? When was the last time I laid eyes on my son, Eva?"

Eva looked briefly away. Harper was right. Seth's mother and stepfather lived in Pennsylvania while Seth lived in Baltimore where he attended John Hopkins University. The only time Harper saw him was when Seth came to Florida during spring break. Even then, Seth didn't spend much time visiting his dad. He was all about having a good time with his friends.

"That's even more reason for us to have our own child. Think about it, Harper. You could be the kind of father that you always wanted. I know it won't make up for what you lost with Seth, but things could be different, in a good way, for you and for me."

Harper responded with silence, disappearing into the bathroom.

Eva didn't give up like she usually did when they discussed having a baby. This time she wanted answers, real answers.

"Harper, don't you walk away from me. Tell me the truth. Are you ever going to change your mind, or are you going to keep hiding behind your son?"

"Don't come to me with that," he yelled. "I don't have to hide behind my son or anyone. You want to know the truth? Well, hear me and hear me good, Eva. We are *not* going to have a baby, so get the idea out of your head. Find yourself a hobby or something and maybe in a couple of years, things will be different."

Eva ran out of the bedroom sobbing, slamming the door behind her.

"Okay, Harper Stenberg, have it your way," she cried as she raced down the stairs. "You don't want me to have your baby then maybe it's time for me to start thinking outside the box."

Chapter 11

"Sometimes who you love isn't who you need." K.
Nola

Seconds after she stepped inside the house, Avery dropped her purse on the end table, kicked off her pumps, and headed straight to the downstairs bathroom. Opening the medicine cabinet, she retrieved the bottle of meds prescribed for depression, opened it, and poured one out in her hand. Next, moving several toiletries aside, she removed a plastic container that looked like a lotion bottle. Opening it, she took out a Xanax and popped it along with the antidepressant into her mouth.

Avery had a doctor she went to see monthly who prescribed Xanax without question. The doctor didn't know that Avery had tried to commit suicide two months prior, and she was not about to be the one to enlighten him. She turned on the faucet at the bathroom sink, cupped her hands underneath the cool water, leaned down, and took a couple of swallows to wash the pills down.

As she stood up, she studied herself in the mirror. She tilted her head from one side to the other, rather slowly. She wasn't conceited, but she considered herself to be an attractive woman. She was confident and she was smart, so why had she been so stupid as to suggest her husband go to bed with her and another woman? She had been drinking that night, and had taken two or three Xanax. That had to be the reason. She wasn't thinking rationally. But no matter whether she had been thinking rationally or not, it was no excuse for Ryker and Olivia to jump in the bed together like two rabbits in heat!

Tears traveled down her face. "Don't you do it," she yelled at the woman staring back at her in the mirror. "Don't you dare cry. No man is worth killing yourself over. No man is worth getting wrinkles over. Straighten up your face, get yourself together."

Avery washed her face then walked out of the bathroom as she began to feel the calming effects of the Xanax.

■

"Mommy, Mommy." Avery heard Lexie and Heather calling her name. "Mommy, wake up," Lexie told her, pushing her back and forth as Avery laid asleep across the sofa in the family room.

She didn't remember dosing off. What time was it anyway? Slowly opening one eye, then the other, she looked at her daughters.

"Hi, there," she said to each of them, sitting up and kissing each one on the forehead. "How was school?"

"It was good," Heather replied.

"Mommy," Mrs. Gates said to ask you if you could pick us up from school tomorrow.

"She has an appointment," Lexie added.

"Sure. No problem. I'll call her later and let her know. It's only one day before it's my carpool day anyway."

"What are you doing home so early?" she asked Ryker as he suddenly walked into the family room.

"I didn't know I had to have permission to come home early."

"Hi, Daddy," Lexie said.

"Hi, sweetheart," he answered. "Hello, munchkin," he said to Heather.

"Hi, Daddy," Heather replied.

Ryker walked over to the girls, kneeled down beside them, and hugged them both.

Avery rolled her eyes at him as she sat all the way upright on the sofa. "Girls, I'll fix you a snack until dinner is ready. Come on," she said to them as she got up off the sofa and sauntered into the open kitchen overlooking the family room.

Lexie and Heather ran ahead of their mother and hopped on the stools in front of the kitchen island.

When Avery looked back, Ryker had disappeared.

Ring. Ring. It was the house phone. She ignored it, knowing that usually whenever the house phone rang, it was someone calling for Ryker.

She was surprised when she heard him on the intercom telling her to pick up the phone. Avery wiped her hands on a dishtowel and went to get the phone sitting on the other end of the kitchen counter.

"Hello," she said into the phone.

"Hi, where's your cell phone? I've been calling you. I was getting worried when you didn't answer."

It was Eva.

"Oh, I left it in my purse, so I didn't hear it. I took a nap after you dropped me off. What's up? You okay?"

"Just went another round with Harper about the same thing. I know you have your own problems, and I don't mean to weigh you down with mine, but you're my best friend. You're the only one I can talk to."

"Listen, I don't want you to feel that you can't talk to me, especially when you know I've had to cry on your shoulder more than I can count." Avery lightly chuckled.

"Meesha and Peyton, they're...well I don't want to hear Meesha's mini-sermons and you and I both know the only time any of us can talk to Peyton is when she's sober."

"Yeah, right...*when* she's sober. How often is that?" Avery laughed into the phone.

"I know, right." Eva laughed too.

"So, what did Harper say this time? I take it he's still against having a baby?" Avery sat a dinner plate with peanut butter, banana, and jelly sandwiches on the island in front of the girls and two cold bottled waters.

"Yes, he's still using the fact that he wasn't a good father as his reason for not wanting me to have a child. It doesn't make sense. Like I told him, I know I would be a good mother. I can take care of a child whether he's at home or not."

"What are you going to do?" Avery asked, leaving the girls in the kitchen and walking back into the family room so they couldn't be all in her conversation.

"I'm thinking about, well, really I'm thinking about going off the pill. I don't have to tell him."

"Do you really think that's a good idea?"

"At this point, I don't care what Harper thinks. I want a baby, Avery. I'm not getting younger so you know what that means. The longer I wait the more difficult it could be for me to get pregnant."

"You're not even thirty yet, so you still have plenty of time. You don't start losing your eggs until you're thirty-five."

"Whose side are you on?" Eva asked.

"Come on now, do you have to ask? I was just saying that you should weigh your options. I don't want things between you and Harper to disintegrate like me and Ryker's relationship."

"I don't think that's going to happen. And as far as you and Ryker, I believe things are going to work out." Eva tried reassuring Avery. "Ryker was terrified when you tried to take your own life. You should have seen him. The man looked like he was going to lose it any

Shelia E. Bell

second. He loves you, Avery. He's just confused, I think.
I don't believe he set out to have an affair. It was only
after—"
"After I put it in his mind. Gosh, I was so stupid. It's
bad enough that he married me knowing about my past.
But to know I had to go and mess things up by practically
forcing him into Olivia's arms—"
"Wait a minute. You didn't force him to do anything.
He made that choice. If he took his marriage as seriously
as you say, there is no way he would have gone to bed
with another woman. You see that he didn't go for having
a threesome, did he?"
"No, he didn't."
"Well, let me say this, just like he said no to the
threesome, he could have said no to going to bed with
her, but he didn't. So stop beating up on yourself. And as
for what you did in your past, I have to admit, I was taken
aback when you said what you said, but that's because of
the way it came out. You just basically blurted it out to
me, Meesha, and Peyton. I was shocked, but I thought
about it after I got home that evening."
"What did you think?" asked Avery.
"I thought about how we all have something we're
hiding. Maybe I haven't been a call girl, but I've done
things in my life that I'm ashamed of. Things I haven't
told anyone. You, at least you were brave enough to trust
us with something so personal."
"I don't know why it just came out, but it did. It's like
I had to release it. I'm tired of hiding, tired of living my
life like I'm on the run or something. That's why I fell for
Ryker so hard."
"I don't understand," said Eva.
"When we met, he knew what I did from the get go,
but still it didn't turn him off. He pursued me knowing
that I was just like those two sisters in the Bible."

58

"What two sisters? What are you talking about?"

"Aholah and Aholibah were their names," answered Avery. "I learned about them a few years ago at a women's retreat Meesha organized. You weren't a member of Perfecting Your Faith then, at least we hadn't met yet."

"I never heard of them."

"They were two whores from the time of their youth all the way up to when they were adults. They even bragged about the many men they had slept with. Then there's another one named Gomer. Gomer was a prostitute when her husband married her. I think his name was….well, I can't remember his name right off, but he said God told him to marry a whore."

"Are you sure all of that's in the Bible?"

"Yes, I'm positive. I'll find where it is and let you know. But either way, I do know Ryker didn't let my profession keep him from pursuing a relationship with me."

"How did you feel about that? I mean, knowing that you were doing what you were doing for a living, and he was part of it too, because he knew you were a call girl. That says to me that he was looking for what you were willing to dish out. Right?" Eva paused on the phone line.

"Stop, Lexie," Heather screamed at her sister, popping her on her hand.

"I didn't do anything," Lexie screamed in return and popped her sister back.

"Get out of here. Go do your homework," Avery ordered her girls.

"Look, girl. We'll talk later. You go on and check on the kids and Ryker, too," Eva insisted.

"Hold up. Eva?"

"Yes?"

"Thanks for not judging me."

"Like I told you, you haven't heard half the stories I could tell you about my life. Buh-bye. We'll talk tomorrow."

"Okay, buh-bye."

Avery stood in the middle of the family room for several seconds, her eyes casted slightly upward. *Lord, I need you.*

Chapter 12

"Children are a gift from God; they are his reward."
Psalm 127:3 TLB

"Honey, why don't you get up and go to your room and lay down if you're sleepy." Peyton stopped at the entrance to Liam's media room when she saw her son slumped back on the sofa with his head lying against the softness of the Italian leather. She noticed quickly that his earplugs, which she could have sworn were a part of his body because he always had them in, were not in his ears. This was totally unlike him because Liam lived and breathed music. There was rarely a time when he wasn't listening to it through his headphones, blasting the music in his media room, or sitting at his small self-made studio making beats. He also entertained many of his friends who enjoyed music too, but there was something different today. Something about Liam that made her question if he was feeling all right. It was a Friday night, and he didn't have any friends over, no music playing, nothing.

Liam didn't respond to her. Peyton walked further into the room until she was standing directly over her son. She touched the top of his head. No response. She shook him.

Liam moaned and slowly raised his head.

Peyton reared back as the smell of alcohol permeated her nostrils.

"You've been drinking!"

Liam looked like he was in a daze. He tried to stand up but stumbled and fell to his knees and onto the hardwood floor.

Before she knew it, Peyton hauled off and started hitting him. Screaming over and over again, she pounded her son as he tried shielding her blows with his hands.

Derek suddenly appeared and grabbed both of her hands, pulling her back and giving Liam a chance to gain his footing.

"What are you doing?" he screamed. "Let him go!"

"He's drunk," she roared as she tried getting out of Derek's vice like grip.

"Stop it, both of you. I'm almost grown. I know what I'm doing. I can handle my own, plus I'm not drunk."

"Oh, so you're saying that the fact that your breath smells like you've had your head buried in a whiskey still doesn't count?"

"I said, I've got this," Derek emphasized again as the phone rang in the background. "Go answer the phone or something. It's probably one of your girls. I know you don't want to miss any of their phone calls," he said sarcastically with a smirk appearing on his bearded face.

The phone stopped ringing. Liam got ready to walk off, but Derek pulled him back. "We aren't finished talking, son."

The phone started ringing again.

The incessant ringing of the phone heightened Peyton's anxiety. She walked off, but not before giving Derek a nasty, evil look.

"Hello," she basically screamed into the phone as soon as she picked it up. Standing in the kitchen with one hand on her hip, she waited for the caller's response.

"I want to see my son."

"Hello?" Peyton said again.

"I want to see my son," the caller repeated.

A shiver ran up and down Peyton's spine. She pulled the receiver from her ear and looked to see the number on the Caller ID. Underneath the phone number, it identified the call as coming from Arizona.

"You have the wrong number."

"Peyton. Don't play with me."

"Who is this?" Peyton asked. "How do you know my name?"

"I'm not calling to start trouble. I just want to see my boy. I want to know if he's okay. Does he play sports? Is he tall? Short? Does he look anything like me?"

Peyton started trembling.

"Mom, I'm sorry," Liam said as he entered the kitchen where Peyton stood at the island.

"Is that my son I hear?" the stranger asked.

Peyton immediately hung up the phone and turned toward Liam. He looked like a little lost and forlorn boy instead of the husky, handsome bushy haired teen that he was.

"Liam…"

The phone rang again. Peyton looked at it as she held it in her hand.

"Aren't you going to answer that?" Liam asked.

"No, what I'm going to do is give my son a hug." She walked up to him, stretched out her arms, and gathered them tightly around him. Her heart was racing and the terror that was building up inside her seemed to almost make her lose her balance.

"Mom, are you okay? You're shaking," Liam said as he stepped out of his mother's arms and looked at her. He was at least half a foot taller than Peyton already, and she was a leggy woman herself.

"I'm fine. Just promise me that you won't drink again, or do any drugs, anything like that ever again. I know I drink too much," she spoke with sadness in her voice. "I have to get myself together, and I promise you from this day forward that I'm going to do better."

Shelia E. Bell

Peyton didn't see Derek standing outside the kitchen. He was taking in every word his wife was saying. Who could blame him? He had voiced more than once to his close friends his discontent with Peyton and her drinking. Maybe she didn't see herself as an alcoholic but Derek begged to differ. He turned to walk off after he heard his son reassuring Peyton that everything was going to be all right.

"It's okay, Mom. I promise I won't do it again. I guess I was just curious. A lot of the kids at school drink. They say it's cool. I was bored, so I decided to see what it was like for myself. It was nasty." Liam made an ugly face.

Smiling, Peyton said, "I love you." She regarded his face, then used the back of her hand to gently stroke the side of it. "No matter what happens, I want you to always remember that."

"Sure, Mom. Now, if you don't mind, I want to go to my room."

"Where's your father?"

We talked but he got a phone call, said he had to go out for a minute."

Peyton folded her arms, inhaled, and pursed her lips. "I see. Well, like I said, I don't want to hear of you doing anything stupid like this again. I can't take it. Do you understand me?"

Liam nodded and exited the room, leaving Peyton standing alone in the middle of the kitchen. She still clutched the phone in her hand, almost jumping when it started ringing again.

"Why are you calling me?" she asked between clenched teeth.

"I want to see my son. I'm going to see my son."

Chapter 13

"It's the friends that you can call up at 4 a.m. that matter." Marlene Dietrich

Meesha found it difficult to maintain her self-composure. She tried to put on her first lady face as she entertained the group of eleven pastors and their first ladies for a dinner party she and Carlton had planned months ago. The annual Pastoral and First Ladies Convention was going to start this Sunday. Since it was being held in Adverse City at the Convention Center, Carlton insisted that they invite some of his pastor friends and associates over for a catered sit down dinner.

At a time such as this, Meesha wished the housewives were with her to give her some much needed support. Even if it meant putting up with Peyton's foolish remarks, or listening to Avery cry about her broken marriage, or seeing the lonely look on Eva's face after telling the housewives that Harper failed to come home again.

Meesha didn't know if she could go through with it. She felt like she would break down at any minute. Chatter was all around her, yet she felt like she was in a room, frozen, dead, and unable to move or speak. She wasn't one to put on a fake smile or pretend like everything was perfect, but tonight she did everything she could to force a smile instead of a frown on her face. She swallowed deeply time and time again to keep herself from bursting into tears.

Surrounded by a sea of so-called men of God, Meesha felt isolated, alone, and frightened. Her mind began to pound her with question after question. *What was she going to do without Carlton? What would the kids do without their father? But most importantly, why did Carlton want out of their marriage? Was God okay with destroying her life?*

"Smile and act normal," she suddenly heard Carlton whisper in her ear. He placed one hand around her tiny waist and kissed her softly on the cheek before raising the glass of sparkling grape juice up to his smiling, deceitful lips.

Was this man bipolar or something? Here he was skinning and grinning, closer to her than a hand in a glove, while just days ago he told her that he wanted his freedom papers.

"What are you doing?" she asked him so that no one could hear her.

"We have a dinner party to get through, people to entertain. You know mostly everyone in this room, so act like it," he ordered through lips that moved like he was a ventriloquist. "We don't air our dirty laundry, so cheer up. You only have a couple of more hours, and this whole evening will be over and done."

Meesha stepped out from the hold of his arm around her waist, and gave Carlton a hateful stare.

"Go to hell!" she snapped, leaving him standing by himself.

She didn't care what Carlton said, nor did she care what any of their guests thought about her, because she was done. She was not going to pretend to be happy when she wasn't. She was a lot of things, but hypocrite was not one of them.

Meesha swiftly left the dinner party and went upstairs. Closing the door to their bedroom, she threw herself on the bed and bawled.

Surprisingly, Carlton didn't come upstairs to see why she had disappeared. Knowing him the way she did, Meesha suspected that he probably hadn't missed her. He was too busy discussing the Bible with his constituents like everything was perfect.

Meesha stopped crying, wiped her eyes with the back of her hands, got up, and walked to the bathroom. Standing in front of the mirror, she stared at her reflection, made a duck lip, then seriously said, "The devil *is* a lie."

Next, she carefully removed her elaborate one of a kind designer gown. She and the housewives had shopped high and low for weeks for the perfect gown for this evening's special event. Out of the dozens of evening dresses she saw, she chose this black textured lace mermaid style gown. It looked ravishing on her. Only tonight instead of feeling like she could out rival any runway model, she felt like she had been made a fool of for all of these years. She needed someone to talk to. She called Eva, but she didn't answer.

Next, she tried calling Avery. When Avery answered the phone, Meesha immediately knew that she had wakened her. She quickly apologized and told Avery she would call her the following day. As she got ready to dial Peyton, the door flew open.

"What do you think you're doing?' Carlton asked. His salmon colored skin looked like it had turned a shade darker. The rise in his voice indicated that he was angry. Carlton was pretty much a laid back kind of man, so when he did get angry or upset, it was easy to tell. But tonight, Meesha could care less whether he was mad or not. He couldn't have it both ways. He wanted out of their marriage, let him be out of it, she reasoned.

"If you think I'm going back down there just so you can save face, then you're sadly mistaken. I don't know why I agreed to still have the dinner party after what you said. I can't do it, Carlton. I'm not going back down there and pretend like all is well in the Porter household when you and I both know that it's far from that."

"Look, you are going to put that dress, that *my* money bought, back on. You are going to come back downstairs. You are going to do whatever you need to do to make sure that our guests feel welcome. You are going to fulfill your role of First Lady. Do you hear me, Meesha?"

"I hear you, Carlton. I hear you loud and clear. But now you listen to me. I am not going down there. I am not going to make you look good one second longer. You're the one who chose to throw our marriage away, so you deal with that decision."

Carlton bit his bottom lip, rolled his eyes up in his head, and flinched his temples. He was definitely at the boiling point. That much Meesha could tell, but she was just as heated.

"I said I am not going back down there. You can go straight to hell, Carlton Porter." Meesha walked off, went to the bathroom, closing and locking the door behind her.

"Meesha, open this door," Carlton yelled as he bammed on the door. "Open this door, get dressed, and get back downstairs. I'm warning you," he threatened.

Meesha ignored Carlton's ranting. She had had enough. She had been his backbone practically since the day the two of them met. She was the one who kept him from breaking when his parents were killed in a terrible car wreck a year after she and Carlton started dating. She was the one who helped him study for his tests while he was in divinity school. She was the one who worked to provide for the two of them so he could concentrate on getting his doctorate in theology. It was her who encouraged him, motivated him, and reminded him of the goals he was trying to reach. Now, he wanted to throw her aside like she was yesterday's garbage, take her children, and walk out? It wasn't going to go down like that. Over her dead body....*or his.*

Chapter 14

"Sometimes the girl who has been there for everyone else needs someone to be there for her." Unknown

"You mean you just left him downstairs with a room full of preachers and their wives? Girl, you can't be serious," Avery said.

"I won't do it. Carlton knows me. He knows I'm not one to fake anything and so do you. So there is no way I can go down there and act like my husband didn't tell me out of the blue that he wants a divorce." Meesha broke down crying. She couldn't fight the hurt anymore.

"Do you want me to come over there?"

"No," Meesha sobbed. 'I'll be fine. God is allowing this for a reason. I don't know what that reason is, Avery, but I have to trust that He has my back."

"I understand what you're saying, but dang, Meesha, you're human. No one can blame you for breaking down. I mean, you and Carlton had the perfect marriage in my eyes. I never in a million years would have ever imagined that the two of you would break up."

"Well, believe it. Because one thing about Carlton; he is not going to say anything that he does not mean."

But that's just it. Something serious has to be going on for him to tell you that he wants out of your marriage. It just doesn't make sense, Meesha. Can you think of anything, and I do mean anything, that can give you some indication as to why he wants to call it quits?"

Avery's mind was going faster than a speeding train trying to come up with one reason after another that the infamous Carlton Porter would want to end his marriage to the world's most perfect woman.

Meesha was a saint in the eyes of Avery and the rest of the housewives, too. Meesha was genuinely a sweet, kind, and compassionate person. She was also a woman of faith. Out of the four housewives, Meesha was the realest.

"I have a mind to go down there and tell everyone to get out of my house."

"What would that solve?" Avery replied. "It's only going to make you look like a raging lunatic. Right now, I bet those first ladies are all down there huddled in a circle whispering, trying to figure out why the first lady of the good pastor of Perfecting Your Faith Ministries suddenly disappeared almost at the beginning of the dinner party. If you feel like you're about to lose it, you really do need to get away from there. Is there some way you can get out of there without anyone seeing you?"

"Have you not heard a word I've said, Avery? I'm not hiding from anyone. I'm not the bad guy here. If I choose to leave out of my house, it will be through whichever door I choose; I don't care who sees me. Let Carlton explain. "

Meesha went over to her bed and lay across it.

"I'll be there in fifteen minutes. "

Avery—"

"Don't try to stop me. I've already picked up my keys and purse; I'm walking toward the door now. I'm calling Peyton and Eva when I get in the car. It's time for an emergency ladies night out. I'll see you in a few. Bye." Avery ended the call.

Meesha removed the phone from her ear, stared at it briefly, and then pressed the END button. She went to her mammoth sized walk-in closet and sifted through literally dozens upon dozens of pants, blouses, and pantsuits. She chose a pair of solid colored slacks and a shirt, pulled a pair of pumps off the shoe shelf, stepped into them then turned and walked out of the closet.

She ventured over to the mirror overlooking the dresser and touched up her hair that was already in a coiled up do. In the bathroom, she washed her face before she touched up the mascara and eyeliner on her marble shaped eyes.

The phone rang just as she was removing contents out of one bag and putting it all inside another.

"I'm on my way downstairs," she told Avery as soon as she answered.

"There you are. We were wondering what happened to you. Are you okay?" the tall, statuesque brunette asked, eyeing Meesha up and down like she was trying to figure out how Meesha had gone from wearing a ravishing evening gown to a pair of slacks and a simple blouse.

"I'm fine, but if you'll excuse me, I'm on my way out. You ladies enjoy yourselves. Have a good time. Make yourself right at home. There is plenty of food, drinks, and entertainment. You won't miss me." She gave the group of women who had gathered next to the first lady, a soft smile, tossed her bag over her shoulder, did a model like turn and walked off like she was cool as a fresh cucumber.

Carlton stood undetected several feet behind the women with his mouth wide open.

"Everything all right?" Reverend Douglas, a minister friend of Carlton's asked, as he walked up on him while peering in the same direction as Carlton. He put a hand on Carlton's shoulder, patting it lightly. "God's word is true, Carlton. What he promises, he will deliver. My brother, I don't know what's going on," he spoke, paused and looked around as if trying to see if anyone was listening. When he was satisfied that no one was, he continued. "But God is our refuge and strength, an ever-present help in trouble." He patted Carlton's shoulder again, but this time with more force behind it.

Carlton nodded. "Everything's good. I'm not worried about a thing. God's word will go on whether we want it to or not, and that goes for His will too."

Carlton looked at Reverend Douglas. "I think it's time for dinner to be served; I sure hope so. I'm famished." He chuckled as he excused himself, departed from Reverend Douglas, and started walking in the direction of the dining area.

Chapter 15

"Nobody is right till somebody is wrong." Unknown

"What happened?" Peyton asked as soon as the door of the SUV opened and Meesha climbed inside. "I know you didn't walk out on your own dinner party?"

Meesha gave Peyton the hand. "Don't start with me, Peyton. I'm not in the mood."

"Lord, have mercy," Peyton mouthed. "The girl does have some backbone." She snickered afterward.

"Are you all right?" asked Avery, eyeing Meesha as she steered the SUV down the street and away from the house.

"I am now that I'm out of there. I know it was probably wrong for me to walk out like I did, but one thing I'm not is fake, and I cannot pretend like everything is wonderful when Carlton has made it clear that he is not happy with me, or this marriage. I just couldn't do it one second longer."

"That's understandable."

"Yeah, I don't blame you," Peyton said.

"Where's Eva?" Meesha asked, looking around the SUV.

"She didn't answer her phone. I called twice. Harper must be at home."

"Humph, that's a miracle," Peyton smarted off. "Where are the boys, Meesha?"

"Carlton, Jr. is spending the night with his best friend. Malik, Marlon, and Micah are next door at the Smithville's."

"Okay, cool. Your kids are taken care of so where are we going?" Peyton asked.

Meesha turned and looked at Peyton who was sitting on the back seat. "Do you really have to ask?"

Peyton's eyebrows rose and she twerked her mouth and shrugged her shoulders. "Please don't tell me we're going there. You know they don't serve alcohol."

"Exactly. So to Diggy's Bistro we go."

Diggy's was a small, private bistro where the girls retreated whenever they wanted to trade in their active lifestyle for private and uninterrupted time together.

The girls drove the rest of the remaining twenty minutes without talking. The radio played one tune after another. Meesha hugged the window as Avery drove.

Meesha thought back on all that had transpired. She reached inside her purse and pulled out her cell phone, and started punching numbers. She called and spoke to her neighbor about her sons. After being reassured that they were fine, she hung up the phone and leaned her head against the windowpane. A fine mist of rain began to silently land on the car. Like she had been hypnotized, Meesha stared intently as the rain gently landed on the window. She imagined that she was like the rain drops falling. Though they couldn't be heard, they could clearly be seen. Though she wasn't physically stating her innermost feelings of betrayal, still hurt was written all over her face. Something had to give. She wanted answers; and she wanted them now.

■

The housewives arrived at Diggy's. Slowly, one by one, they got out of the SUV. Once inside, they were greeted by a hostess and led to a table toward the middle of the bistro.

Sitting at the table, Peyton reached over and took hold of Meesha's hand. "We're not going to let you go through this alone. I hope you know that."

Meesha nodded. "Thanks." She looked over at Peyton who was sitting across from her. "Thanks, Peyton. I don't know what I would do without you guys."

"Like the song goes, *that's what friends are for*," Peyton sang off key.

The three of them talked for the next couple of hours until Meesha decided it was time to pick up her boys and head back home. After going back and forth with Peyton and Avery, she determined that it wasn't her who had anything to run from. She shouldn't have left her own home tonight. If anybody should have felt uncomfortable hosting the dinner party, it should have been Carlton. He was the hypocrite - not her.

All the way back to Meesha's house Avery and Peyton continued to give Meesha a dose of her own words of encouragement. They reminded her of the faith and trust she always exuded and how she was the one who told them to pray about everything.

This was one of those times when Meesha needed to hear her very words being hurled back at her; not in a mean or spiteful manner, but in the kind, loving way Avery and yes, even Peyton displayed.

Meesha arrived at her neighbor's house. She gathered up her three boys, got back in the SUV and Avery drove them home.

"Thanks again for everything," Meesha said to Avery and Peyton as she and her sons got out of the SUV. "Boys, go on up to the house. I'm right behind you." She focused back on what she was about to say to Avery and Peyton. "If it hadn't been for the two of you coming to rescue me from all this madness tonight, I don't know what I would have done. I felt like I was about to explode."

"But you didn't," Peyton said, smiling slightly.

"Looks like all of your guests have left," Avery said as she looked at the empty driveway that was filled to the brim with cars when they first arrived. There weren't even any cars parked on the side of the street. "Guess the coast is clear."

"Thank you, God," Meesha said as she quickly looked upwards at the dark star-lined sky.

Meesha looked over her shoulder. Her sons were standing on the wraparound porch waiting for her to finish talking.

"Goodnight. I love you," Meesha said to both Peyton and Avery.

"Love you too," Avery answered.

"Me too," Peyton added. "Now go on inside. We'll talk to you tomorrow."

"Here I come, boys," Meesha said as she trotted toward the steps leading up to the front entrance and onto the porch.

She had no idea what Carlton was going to say, but at this point, she didn't care. He was the one big on wanting to make others think that his life was picture perfect. Just a few days ago, if someone had told her that it was anything different, she would have boldly called them a lie, but even *she* had been duped.

Chapter 16

"Any relationship which starts with a lie will end with a truth." *Anurag Prakesh Ray*

Walking inside the lavish house, all was relatively quiet. Meesha went toward the kitchen and dining area. It appeared that everyone was gone, except the remaining caterers who were cleaning up. She sighed in relief.

"Go upstairs, get your baths, and get ready for bed," she ordered the boys who trailed right behind her. Without so much as saying a word, they did what their mother told them.

She remained at the bottom of the stairs, for no apparent reason, and watched the boys until they disappeared.

"You satisfied with yourself?"

Meesha turned around at the sound of Carlton's voice. She could tell from his tone that he was angry.

"Actually," she said folding her arms together, "no, I'm not and I won't be satisfied until you tell me what's going on with you."

"Humph. You think embarrassing me in front of my peers is the way to make me talk? I can't believe you could be so selfish." His voice rose an octave.

Meesha was relatively surprised at his tone because Carlton was known to be a low key, soft-spoken man. Tonight Meesha was hearing and seeing a side of him she'd seen very few times during their marriage, and she didn't like it.

"Me," she pointed to herself, "embarrassed you?" She chuckled. "You can't be serious. You expect me to act like the perfect first lady when just days ago you told me you no longer wanted to be married," Meesha retorted.

The force in her voice indicated her own rising anger. "I don't know who you think I am, Carlton Porter, but I'm telling you this; I am not going to be tossed to the side like I'm nothing. I've given you a good marriage, bared your children, stood by you through your dreams, not mine, yours, Carlton."

"So what you're saying is that you never wanted to be my first lady? You never wanted to be a preacher's wife?" he barked.

Meesha turned briefly and glanced upstairs, making sure that the boys were still inside their rooms. "If you want to talk sensibly about this, let's go in the study. I don't want the boys to know that their father is a first class jerk who's ready to walk out of their lives." Meesha walked away from the stairs, pass Carlton, down the corridor, and toward the study.

"I would never walk out on my kids. You know that, so don't even go there, Meesha. This has nothing to do with the boys. I love my kids."

Meesha opened the door to the study and walked inside with Carlton following her and closing the door behind them.

"You just don't love their mother," she said as she told herself not to cry.

"That's what you're saying, not me."

"Who is she? Was she here tonight? Was she in my house, Carlton?"

"I don't know what you're talking about."

"Stop playing me for the fool. What other reason can you give me that would make a man walk away from his ministry, his wife, his children, everything that we've built together. Now tell me, who is she?"

"There is no other woman. And as far as my ministry goes, I said nothing about leaving the ministry. God called me to preach and that's what I plan on doing until the day I die."

"How are you going to stand in a pulpit Sunday after Sunday living a lie? Have you told your so-called peers your plans?"

Carlton was quiet. He looked away and walked to the right of him toward the built-in shelves containing rows of books, mostly religious.

"You haven't told them, have you? What's going on with you? Talk to me, Carlton." Meesha's voice suddenly became soothing as she realized that her husband was keeping his decision from everyone. "This isn't like you. Tell me what's really going on. Please."

Carlton stood staunch in front of the wall of books, refusing to look at his wife. How could he tell her the truth? What was he supposed to do? What was he supposed to say?

So this is how it's going to be, huh? Well, have it your way, Carlton. I'm done. I won't go through this kind of anguish. I won't do it and I don't deserve it," she said and stormed out of the study.

Chapter 17

"My yesterdays walk with me. They keep step, they are gray faces that peer over my shoulder." William Golding

Peyton drove toward the other side of town, a less than favorable neighborhood of Adverse City, but she had to do what she had to do because there was no way on God's green earth she was going to let the woman come to her house.

Her hands trembled slightly as she gripped the steering wheel. Biting her bottom lip, she prayed aloud inside the car. "Lord, fix it. Don't let this blow up in my face."

She drove several miles into the neighborhood, listening to the navigation system as it directed her to the location of the restaurant where she had agreed to meet Breyonna.

Her past was like a nightmare. It returned day in and day out, haunting her, never fully allowing her to live in her present. Why now, after all these years, had Breyonna decided to track them down?

Peyton slowly pulled into the parking lot of the small hole in the wall restaurant, parked her car, and waited inside of it for a few minutes before she sucked in a deep breath, opened the car door, and with feet that felt like lead, she went inside to confront her past head on.

Inside the restaurant, her feet made a smacking sound as she fought to walk across the tiled floor that gripped the bottom of her shoes like super glue. All eyes seemed to fixate on her as she scanned the small restaurant until her eyes focused in on a woman sitting midway the restaurant in a booth. She had golden locks of curly blonde hair that kissed the top of her shoulders. Their eyes locked and the woman smiled, raising her hand slightly toward Peyton. Looking around, uncertain if the woman was calling for her, Peyton saw that the strangers in the restaurant were still gawking.

She suddenly realized that her designer pantsuit, signature pumps and handbag, $200 hairdo and the giant rock on her ring finger must have been what made her the center of attention. She felt quite nervous, and irritated at herself, that she hadn't dressed down. Dang, what she wouldn't give for a drink. She ignored the stares and the catcall from a black male with a humongous piece of jewelry draping his neck, and a hat pulled half way down over his head. A man sitting across from him laughed as she passed by.

Lord, help me get through this, she prayed as she walked toward the woman.

"Breyonna?"

"How soon we forget," the woman remarked snidely.

Peyton sat across from her in the booth. There was a glass half filled with soda sitting on the table with a plate of half eaten fries next to it.

"I'm not here to play games with you," Peyton immediately said as she sat her purse next to her, with her arm looped inside the straps of it, like she was trying to make sure it was secured.

"What makes you think I'm here to play games? I want to see my son. Point blank. Now, tell me when we can make that happen."

"*Your* son?" Peyton chuckled, throwing her head back. Next, she pushed back her bangs from off of her flawlessly made-up oval face. Scouring she said, "How dare you come here after not having seen or tried to contact us for the past thirteen years of his life. The boy doesn't know you and frankly, I don't want him to know you. You think you can just waltz in town, intrude on my life, and demand to see my son. Well, let me say this," she fumed, pointing her finger at the woman. "You don't scare me. Now, tell me, how much do you want this time, Breyonna?"

Peyton looked down at her side at her purse, opened it, and pulled out her wallet.

Breyonna's glare was sharp enough to cut through bulletproof glass. "Hah, you think I want money?"

"Why else would you be here? Why would you show up in Adverse City after all of these years demanding to see the little boy that I," she pointed at herself, "have raised to be the outstanding young man that he is."

"Because when it's all said and done, he's *my* son. You don't have any right to him. Let's be real here, Peyton. You think that changing his name and giving him a new identity would change the truth? You thought leaving Memphis would keep me from finding you? I guess you see that I'm too smart for you, huh? I was always one step ahead of you, high or not. And no matter what name you call him, it does not make him belong to you," Breyonna seethed. "You didn't give birth to him; I did. So I suggest you not push me, Peyton."

Peyton put her wallet back inside her purse. "Don't you threaten me." She leaned in toward Breyonna from across the booth. "You were the one strung out on heroin. You were the one who gave him away. If it hadn't been for me, God only knows if he would still be alive."

Breyonna shook her head then began to clap. "Bravo, what an act. You want thanks, I'll give you your thanks. I appreciate what you did to help me out. But look at me." Breyonna regarded herself. "Do I look like I'm that person from all those years ago? I've cleaned up my act.

I've been clean and sober, unlike some folks I know," she snarled, "for the past couple of years."

Peyton frowned. "Oh, so that makes you a mother now? That gives you the right to disrupt Liam's life. He's not some puppy dog, not some toy that you toss back and forth, Breyonna. Now, tell me how much you want?"

"Let's see what his father thinks about this."

"His father? Are you kidding me? How many men will have to line up for that DNA test?"

This time Breyonna leaned in, balled up her fist, and pounded the wobbly table. It shook like a tiny earthquake. "Yes, his father, his d-a-d-d-y. I may have been on heroin back then, but I know who my baby daddy is. It's Carlton Porter. And I know where he is. I've even been in touch with him."

"You're such a liar. You tried to feed me that crap about Carlton being Liam's daddy, when you and I both know that's another one of your bold faced lies."

"What make believe world are you living in, Peyton? Look, you say you don't have time for games; well neither do I. I want to see my son. I'll give you a few days, a week at the longest to tell him that his dear, sweet mother is in town. I'll call you and make arrangements to see my son. As for Carlton, he is definitely his father and he knows the truth. Believe that!"

"Get out of my face or I won't be responsible for what I do to you!" Peyton screamed back.

Breyonna stood up with such force that the booth table shook again, slightly moved, and almost pinned Peyton against the back of the wooden bench. "You've got one week." A tired looking waitress approached the table. "She's got the check," Breyonna told her, walking off and leaving out of the restaurant.

"Give me a shot of vodka," Peyton practically ordered the chunky, gold-toothed, senior citizen looking waitress. "On second thought, make that a double."

Chapter 18

"What's money? A man is a success if he gets up in the morning and goes to bed at night and in between does what he wants to do." Bob Dylan

Eva stood outside leaning on her bedroom balcony, inhaling the crisp, spring air. The sun was bright; the soothing perfect breeze kissed her skin. The view of the ocean was visible in the horizon.

Harper came up behind, startling her somewhat. Embracing her from behind, he nuzzled her on her neck. "You aren't still upset with me are you?"

Eva tensed up. She didn't respond nor did she move.

Harper kissed her on the back of her neck. Moving her hair aside, he planted butterfly kisses from shoulder to shoulder.

Eva felt both excited and aggravated as Harper slowly turned her around. Almost immediately, the tension disappeared from her face when she turned to him.

"I love you, Eva. I know you want us to have a child, but not right now. Just be patient with me, sweetheart."

She stiffened momentarily, as she shuddered inwardly at the thought of again having to wait to get pregnant. Her frustration didn't last long as she became entranced by the chocolate of his eyes.

With his powerful hands, he pulled her to him, leaving no space between them. His lips pressed against hers as he moved his mouth over hers hungrily, and his tongue explored the recesses of her mouth.

She kissed him back as she succumbed to him. Her knees weakened as she drank in the sweetness of his kiss and felt his desire separated only by his boxer briefs.

Without missing a beat, he walked her backwards into their bedroom while Eva's emotions whirled and the blood pounded in her brain.

His hand moved under her Victoria's Secret nightie to skim her hips and thighs. The gentleness of his touch sent currents of desire racing through her.

Gently, he eased her down onto the bed. She moaned softly as he laid her down.

The sound of the doorbell rudely intervened.

"Who could that be?" she said in as reasonable a voice as she could manage.

"I don't know," Harper answered in a hoarse whisper.

The doorbell chimed again.

Harper got up, grabbed his robe from off the headboard, and went downstairs to see who the culprit was that was responsible for stopping him from making love to his wife.

His voice was stern as he walked down the foyer and to the front door, as the doorbell rang a third time. "Who is it?" Harper opened the door and there stood Seth.

Eva halted, dressed scantily in her matching silk thigh length robe. She had yet to meet Harper's son. She'd only seen him on pictures and a time or two when she passed by Harper while he video chatted with him. For the brief moments she saw him standing in front of his dad, Seth had an uncanny resemblance to his father, only he was a younger version.

Eva brushed her hair from off her face and stepped back, her breath suddenly short. For a split second, Seth's gaze deflected to her and their eyes did a dance before she hurriedly turned and took off back up the steps to get fully dressed.

On her way back downstairs after slipping into a black and white stripe maxi dress, Eva paused and listened. The muffled sounds of a heated discussion caused her to walk slowly in the direction of the voices. She could tell they were coming from the library. As she drew closer, she heard Harper's escalated voice.

"You drop out of school and think you're just going to show up here like it's nothing? All the money I've spent on you and this is how you repay me?"

"That's all you think about; money, money, money. You haven't bothered to ask me why I dropped out. But you don't care about that, do you?" Seth bit back, sounding just as angry as his father.

"I know what it better not be; some grandiose idea that you can make a living in the music industry. "

"You know what, Dad, it's not some grandiose idea. I love music; you know this. You've always known this about me. I'm not like you. I don't want to be a doctor."

The door to the library was slightly ajar. Eva planted herself on the opposite side of the door to avoid detection. She continued listening as father and son went back and forth, each adamant about how they felt about the situation. Eva could understand Seth's sentiments. From what Harper told her, Seth was a talented musician and songwriter. But she also understood that Harper really wanted his son to follow in his medical footsteps.

"I'm not you, and I don't want to be you. All I'm asking for is your support of something that I know I was meant to do. Just like you know you were meant to be a doctor, why can't you understand that I was meant to touch lives through my music?"

Eva heard the tone soften in Harper's voice as he seemed to finally hear what Seth was saying.

"You know what, maybe you're right. You do have your own dreams to fulfill. Who am I to shove mine down your throat? Tell you what I'll do. The money I was going to pay for the next year of college tuition for you, I'll invest in your music," Harper said in a totally different tone.

Eva leaned against the wall and smiled. Harper was a great person, a good father, and in spite of the fact that he spent more time away from home than at home, and he didn't want another kid right now, she still would say that he was a good husband.

"You won't be sorry, Dad. Oh, and there's one more thing I wanted to ask," she heard Seth say.

"What's that, son?"

"Can I camp out in the guest house for a few months? I promise I'll do whatever I need to do, get a part-time gig, wait tables, whatever I have to do to support myself while I do this thing."

"Sure. I see making *The Alchemist* required reading really did pay off," Harper said to his son, followed by a short deep chuckle.

Eva stood straight up, turned around, and swiftly walked up the hall before either of them could come out and catch her eavesdropping. With a smile on her face, she went outside in the back yard. Standing on the outdoor covered lanai, she sucked in the fresh Florida air, looked toward the sky, and smiled. "God, thank you for working things out. If you worked it out between Harper and Seth, I know you're going to work things out between me and Harper. All you have to do is give me a baby.

Chapter 19

"Friendship is born at that moment when one person says to another: "What! You too? I thought that no one but myself..." C. S. Lewis

"So, this was your first time meeting Harper's son?" Peyton asked as she and Eva talked on the phone while Peyton was on her way to today's ladies' day out. "Is he as fine as his daddy?" Peyton teased.

Eva, en route too, steered down Adverse Boulevard toward Bianca, another exclusive, celeb central spot inside the Delano Hotel where the housewives often dined. "I don't understand you sometimes."

"What is it you don't understand?"

"You can be so superficial. Is that all you can think to ask is how fine he is?"

There was a moment of silence between the phone lines.

"Hello," Eva spoke louder inside her car, thinking that she may have lost her connection with Peyton.

"I'm here."

"Oh, I thought I'd lost the call. You weren't saying anything."

"I'm waiting on you."

"Waiting on me to what?"

"Answer my question. Is he as fine as his daddy?"

Eva laughed over the phone this time. "Peyton Hudson, I don't know what to say about you, except I can't help but love you. So, to answer your question, girl, yes, the boy is *fiiine*!

The women both laughed this time as Eva made a left turn followed by a quick right into the valet parking area of the hotel.

With the four of them gathered together, almost immediately they began to talk about the latest news they wanted to share with each other. There wouldn't be too much that Eva and Avery hadn't already shared with one another during the course of the week, seeing that they talked almost every day. Surprisingly, however, Eva hadn't told Avery about her stepson popping up on her doorstep the day before.

"Are you sure Harper is cool having his grown son living there? I mean, you said that he hardly visited before, and he never lived with Harper full time, so what kind of adjustment is it going to be for Harper?" asked Meesha.

"For Harper? You mean me, don't you? Think about it, what does Harper have to worry about? He's not home half the time, and Seth is going to be staying in the guest house."

"Still, the fact that another person is going to be living on your property does make a difference," added Avery.

"What did Harper say to you? Did he even discuss it with you to see how you felt about his son appearing out of nowhere and now all of a sudden he's taken up residence in your home? I don't think I could deal with it," Peyton said. "I don't care how fine he is."

Meesha remained quiet. She sipped on a hot cup of Red Robe tea, apparently choosing to keep her opinions about Eva's dilemma to herself. Perhaps she felt that she had no room to dabble in anyone else's problems when she had enough of her own.

"What do you think about it?" asked Eva.

"Huh?" Meesha replied, placing the cup back down on its saucer.

"I said, what do you have to say about Seth living with me and Harper for a few months?"

Shelia E. Bell

"He *is* Harper's son; he's an adult so it's not like you have to change his diapers and keep his nose clean."

The three housewives suddenly stopped their chatter and all eyes zoomed in on Meesha.

"What?" Meesha asked, looking curiously back at each them. "Why are you looking at me like that?"

"Because," Peyton said, being the first one to speak up, which of course was definitely not unusual for Peyton. "You don't have anything to say about praying and asking God for guidance. You know all of that stuff you always say when one of us is going through something."

"Of course, praying and asking God for guidance is a given, but," Meesha looked directly at Eva, "I shouldn't have to tell you that, right?"

"Well, I can't say that I prayed about it. I mean, think about it. He just popped up yesterday. I haven't had time to think about what I feel, how to react, and definitely I haven't thought about going to God. I'm just telling you what God loves: the truth."

"That's understandable, but you don't need to put matters off. Pray about it, go to Harper - today. I don't care if you have to go see him at the hospital; go and talk to your husband. He needs to tell you something. You're his wife. You deserve to be part of the decision to bring someone into your household."

Avery nodded her head in agreement. "She's right about that."

"You're a wise woman, Meesha."

Meesha blushed. "Peyton, do not humor me."

"I'm not humoring you. I'm serious." Peyton didn't crack a smile as she spoke. Her voice almost sounded on the verge of breaking down, like she was about to cry. Her face turned red and her bubbly laughter was nowhere to be found.

"What's going on with you?" asked Meesha. "This doesn't sound like you. You look like you just saw a ghost."

"I can't talk about it. I wish I could, but I can't."

"Yes you can," Eva spoke up. "If we can air our dirty laundry to you Lady TMZ," Eva chortled, "I know you should have no problem telling us what's going on with you."

Peyton shook her head, picked up her cosmopolitan and took two swallows. "When I can tell you, I will." She spoke in a soft whisper.

"I don't like the way you sound." Avery, sitting on the right side of Peyton, patted her on the back. "Are you sure you're okay?"

"I'm good. Seriously, I'll tell you when I can. Now stop giving me the third degree." She looked at each one of her friends and gave them the old Peyton stare down.

"Well, if you want to talk, I'm here for you," Meesha said.

Peyton looked at Meesha with a look of discomfort in her eyes. She hated to keep her secret from Meesha, or the other housewives, but until she could talk to Carlton herself, there was no way she was going to divulge anything. Breyonna couldn't have really confronted Carlton or had she? Was Breyonna the reason Carlton asked Meesha for a divorce and if so, what was he planning to do about Liam? And why hadn't he said anything to her?

"That includes me," said Eva, interrupting Peyton's thoughts. "We're all here for you."

"It goes without any of us saying, but I'll say it anyway, no matter what it is, we are the Housewives of Adverse City and we stick together," Avery chimed. "Now raise your glasses.

They did.

"To friendship everlasting," said Avery.
"To friendship everlasting," the rest of them repeated.

■

After spending the afternoon with the housewives, Peyton left the hotel restaurant and headed home. On the way, she called Liam on his cell phone to see if he was still at his best friend, Paul's house. He was. He told her that he would be home later that afternoon. Being that it was the weekend, Peyton didn't mind if Liam wanted to hang out with his friends.

"Hey, there," Derek greeted her almost as soon as she walked inside the house and up the hallway toward their bathroom.

Peyton looked up and around and faced Derek. "Hi."

"How was your girls' day out?"

"Good," she said nonchalantly. "Why the sudden interest in how my day has been?"

"See, there you go. When I try to talk to you, this is what I get." He turned and started walking away.

"Hold up. I'm sorry. It's just that we hardly ever talk anymore. And for you to ask about my afternoon, well, it caught me off guard. It was good. How was your day?"

They stood in the hallway at least a few feet apart from one another as they talked.

"Busy, not that I'm complaining."

Peyton smiled. Derek, despite her accusing him of using her for her money, was a self-made millionaire. She would tell him early in their marriage that he should be sitting on the team of Shark Tank; he was just that shrewd in business. Derek developed and launched an app when he was fresh out of high school. The app became so successful that he sold it several years ago to a leading tech company for millions of dollars. From what

Peyton had come to learn over the years, Derek's older brother and his grandfather were well respected investment bankers and financial wizards in their hometown of Jacksonville where his family still lived, though they never reached the level of financial success as Derek. Derek always wanted more. He reveled in the status and respect he had achieved, and the amount of fame and fortune that had come along with having a boat load of money and means. Peyton wasn't one to complain about his busy lifestyle because it afforded her to live a life that she had been accustomed to growing up as a child of privilege. She wanted that for Liam, too. She also wanted her parents to be proud of her, that she had married a man who was just as dogmatic about being successful and rich as her father had been.

When she met Derek, there's was a whirlwind romance. They met and dated for less than a year when he proposed and she readily accepted. It was love at first sight for the both of them. Derek didn't mind that she had a son. Peyton told Derek she adopted the boy shortly after both of his parents were killed in a car accident.

When they got married, Derek wanted to adopt Liam as his own, but Peyton always balked at the idea, determined to keep the discovery of her son's true identity a secret. That period of her life and marriage was troubling for Peyton. She prayed day in and day out that Derek would not discover that Liam's birth records had been falsified. As bad as she hated to admit it, and she never had, she used the social security number of her deceased uncle. Unlike Liam's make believe daddy, her Uncle Gary really did die in a car accident.

Now with the sudden appearance of Liam's biological mother, Peyton was terrified. How would Liam react if she was forced to tell him the truth; that he was not her biological son? And then there was her marriage. Derek would definitely implode if he discovered she had been lying to him all of these years. Her marriage would be over if her lies were exposed. There were already times when Derek threatened to leave her because he thought she drank too much, but thank God, he never had. But to find out something like this? Peyton realized that no amount of pleading or I love you's or promises to stop drinking would save her.

Derek was one of the good guys. He worked hard but he also liked to play hard. There used to be a time that she liked to play hard right along with him, accompanying him to high society social events. Going to formal dinners, the symphony orchestra, the ballet, live theatre, ballroom dancing, and co-mingling with some of the bigwig account holders at Adverse City Bank, were all the kinds of things Derek enjoyed.

Slowly over the years, things had changed, at least they'd changed on her end. As for Derek, he still played hard, only most of the time it was without Peyton hanging on to his arm.

Peyton shuttered like a cup of ice water had been poured down her back as she thought about how she had embarrassed him some years back. They were at a charity event hosted by one of Derek's filthy rich associates at a private golf country club on Fisher Island. She hadn't intended to drink as much as she had that evening. Everything happened so fast. She and Derek danced, mixed, mingled, and rubbed elbows with money - money that made their millions look like pennies. The drinks kept appearing from out of nowhere, and Peyton wasn't one to turn down the offer of a good stiff drink.

How was she supposed to remember being so inebriated that she walked into the wife of one of Derek's associates with such force that the woman lost her balance and fell to the floor with Peyton landing on top of her. From what Derek told her, she couldn't get up off the floor. People gathered around to help her and the woman up off the floor, only to have Peyton fall back down as soon as they helped her to her feet. She was so drunk that Derek had to shamefully excuse himself, and her, from the event. Since that time, Peyton could count the times Derek invited her to events like that. But that was nothing, compared to this thing with Breyonna. There was no way on God's green earth that Derek would ever forgive her. He based his life on being honest and trustworthy and Peyton was neither.

Chapter 20

"And let us not neglect our meeting together, as some people do." NLT Bible (Hebrews 10:25)

A guest preacher delivered the Sunday message. He wasn't half as good as Carlton. If she had to grade him, Meesha would give him a C.

Meesha, and the housewives, along with Derek and Ryker lined the second church pew. The wide brimmed Sunday hats the housewives wore blocked the view of probably six or seven rows of people planted behind them.

Eva sat next to Meesha. Again, Harper was missing in action. He'd gotten a call from the hospital at the crack of dawn, got up, dressed in his scrubs, and headed out the door before the sun peeked from behind the clouds.

Avery adjusted her stylish hat and then laid her hand on top of Ryker's hand. Did she feel him stiffen at her touch? She told herself to ignore it and enjoy the fact that he was at church with her. Worshipping the Lord on Sunday morning, as Ryker called it, was a given. Being raised by parents who took him and his siblings to church every Sunday and two times during the week, Ryker felt Sunday mornings belonged to God. Avery tightened her grasp on Ryker's hand as she leaned in and looked over at their daughters. A smile of satisfaction appeared on her face. *Save my relationship, dear Lord,* she prayed to herself.

Peyton was glad she made the decision to wear a wide-brimmed hat that swooped down in the front, partially shielding the fear she was sure could be detected in her eyes. She stood with the rest of the congregation as they recited the church declaration. Closing her eyes, she saw an image of Breyonna standing in front of her threatening to take Liam away. A tug on her hand brought her out of her daydream. She opened her eyes as Derek eased the Bible between the two of them to read the passage of scripture along with the preacher and the rest of the congregation.

Peyton looked at the passage that she'd seen and read numerous times before. Today, it came to life for her, but instead of helping her, it increased her worries. "For God gave us a spirit not of fear but of power and love and...." She heard Derek and the other housewives reading. Her heart muscles tightened like octopus tentacles. *What if I lose my baby? What if she comes and takes Liam away from me?* She felt her body grow limp but there was nothing she could do about it. It was almost like one of those out of body experiences that she'd heard people talking about on television.

"Are you all right?" she heard Derek whisper in her ear at the same moment his arm wrapped around the backside of her waist, steadying her.

"Yes," she whispered back. "Just a little lightheaded." She slowly sat down on the pew. Derek followed.

The remaining congregation sat down at the end of the scripture reading. Peyton looked up and caught Avery staring at her. "You all right?" Avery mouthed without saying the words aloud.

Peyton nodded.

"You want me to take you home?" Derek asked.

"No, I'm fine. Probably stood up too fast and the blood rushed to my head. I'm good now," she convinced Derek. If only it was that easy to convince herself.

■

Avery volunteered to take Meesha's kids home with her after church. She was taking Lexie and Heather to get pizza and decided to make a small party out of it. Meesha's boys loved to hang around Avery because she had a way with kids.

Carlton and Meesha drove home alone in silence. When they walked inside the house, Carlton laid his Bible on the table in the family room, removed his Tom Ford suit jacket, and loosened his tie as he made the trek upstairs.

Silence lingered.

Meesha went upstairs too, taking off her hat as she climbed the winding staircase. If Carlton wanted to give her the silent treatment because of the decision *he* made, then so be it. She was hurt but she was not one to beg, never had been, and she wasn't about to start now. She would keep praying and relying on God to work things out.

Inside their bedroom, they both undressed. Meesha changed out of her chic fit and flare dress and put on her robe. Tying the belt tightly around her petite waist, she put on a pair of her favorite shoes, some multi-colored clogs.

Carlton was still getting undressed when Meesha left him in the room and went back downstairs.

Downstairs and in the kitchen, she looked inside the refrigerator and removed the containers of food that Yulisa had prepared for today's dinner. Yulisa was off on Sundays and some Saturdays, so she made sure the family had full course meals prepared that only needed warming up or minor prepping.

Meesha paused for a minute when she heard Carlton coming downstairs. She listened as his footsteps told her that he was going toward his study.

Opening each container and examining the delectable looking dishes, she started to fix herself a plate, but then stopped and left out of the kitchen, leaving the containers sitting on the counter.

This was not going to keep going on the way that it was. Carlton was going to have to tell her something and he was going to have to tell her today. This silent treatment was for the birds and she wasn't having it.

She opened the door of the study. Carlton was at his desk staring out the picture window at the landscaped yard that they paid an arm and a leg to a gardener to maintain. Inside the door with arms folded, she boldly asked, "When are you leaving? I mean, why do you want to stay here if you want a divorce so badly?"

Carlton didn't respond, at least not with words.

When he looked at her, Meesha could swear it looked like the man had been crying. But if that was the case, why? He's the one who wanted out of the marriage.

Carlton pushed back from the mahogany desk, got up, and like superman in a leap and a bound, he was less than a foot away.

"You're so dang sexy."

Meesha frowned. What was he doing? Playing with her? Toying with her heart?

Another small step and Carlton stood in front of her. Without saying another word, he grabbed her into his arms, using one hand to close the door to the study and pushing her against it. Slowly, yet with firmness, her body was sandwiched between him and the wall while he voraciously kissed her. His hands played her body like she was a fine tuned instrument. His breathing was hard and rough, as he seemed like he could devour her.

As badly as she wanted to push him away, she couldn't. Carlton was an expert lover and their sex life was never lacking. But why now? How could he be kissing her and touching her this way if he was so unhappy with her? She was growing more confused by

101

the minute. She slightly nudged him as her mind tried to ask the questions her body didn't care about.

"You...want," she tried talking, but his touch, his kisses, his warm breath against her neck rendered her speechless.

Carlton's tongue cut off her breath. She gasped when his hand went underneath her robe. He loosened the belt on it and gained total access to her.

After their steamy lovemaking, Meesha was left weak and trembling. Tears rolled down her cheeks as she turned to walk out of the study.

"Hold up. Where are you going?"

Meesha looked at him. "What kind of games are you playing? I don't understand you. You tell me the truth, or you can pack your bags and leave right now. I won't let you use me for your own selfish satisfaction. Whoever it is you're divorcing me for, I suggest you go to her to get your rocks off."

With that being said, Meesha stormed out of the study. She hurried upstairs to their bedroom, and went straight to the bathroom. Closing the door behind her, she allowed the flood of tears to flow as she turned on the shower and stepped underneath the jets of warm streaming water. Her body heaved as she cried for the demise of life the way she'd known it. Where had things gone wrong? Maybe Carlton was going through some kind of crisis or maybe he was ill. He was willing to lose his family, possibly his church, and all for some other woman. It didn't make sense.

Carlton decided against following her, and instead went into one of the guest bathrooms downstairs, where he took a quick shower. With a towel draped around his Adonis body, he went into the kitchen. Containers filled with food were laced across the countertop next to the refrigerator. Meesha had obviously taken them out of the fridge with the intent of warming it up.

He looked inside each container. After getting a plate from the overhead cabinet, he began placing food onto his plate, and then warmed it in the microwave. Sitting down to eat, he prayed first before diving into his food. While eating, he remembered that he'd left his phone in the study. He got up, went to retrieve it, and while on his way back to the kitchen, it started ringing. Looking at it, he hesitated then pushed Ignore. The phone started ringing again. Again, he pushed Ignore.

Sitting back down at the table, Carlton stroked his smooth bald head. His text message notifier chimed.

"u can run but u cant hide. Answer da phone."

Carlton read the text message and replied. "busy."

"need to see u."

"Impossible."

"Nothing impossible. I need to see u or mayb it's ur wife I need to b talkin to."

"Leave her out of this."

"Meet me n 30 min @ Adverse City Park."

Carlton got back up from the table and went upstairs to get dressed. He'd had enough. It was time to handle this situation once and for all.

Chapter 21

"Sin has many tools, but a lie is the handle which fits them all." Oliver Wendell Holmes

"How much do you want?"

"Who says it's your money I want? Why don't we try to make a go of this? I'm clean and sober. I want to make things right. I need you to believe me," Breyonna sat next to him on a bench at the lake.

It was a perfect day. The weather was delightful, the sun beamed, but not too hot. The park was bustling with life.

"That's it, I don't believe you. I haven't seen or heard from you in years. You think you can just show up here and invade my life, not to mention your son's life. Have you ever stopped once to think how it would affect him if he found out that I'm his father? That is, if I really am his father."

"Oh, you're his daddy all right. You know it and I know it. I've loved you since college and you know it. I thought you loved me, too. Why else would I keep sleeping with you whenever you came to Memphis."

"Stop it already. You're delusional. Who's to say how many men you've slept with since you got on that horse and went mad," Carlton said.

"Well, I'm not on anything now. I've been clean for a while. And I know it can work between us. I know it can. Our son is old enough to understand that people make mistakes. I did what I thought was best for him back then. I told you that you had a kid, but because I was strung out, you didn't believe me. I know I stayed too high to think straight. But Peyton could have convinced you. She could have told you who he was just as easily as I did. It's not like I didn't tell her whose kid he was."

"You're lying. I don't believe Peyton would keep something like this from me for all this time, that is if she suspected that the boy was really mine."

"Well, you better believe it. You and I both know that Peyton has always been nothing but a selfish, think she so mighty, witch," remarked Breyonna. "She couldn't have you, so I guess she kept the boy all to herself. She was so in love with you back in college, so since you didn't feel the same way, maybe she thought our kid would give her some solace. Who knows what she's thought all these years, and who gives a rat's behind anyway. I know I don't. All I'm here for is my kid. I could care less about Peyton and her feelings."

Carlton looked at her with disgust flowing from his eyes. "You're the one who traded him to her for a thousand bucks, so I wouldn't be so quick to throw Peyton under the bus. Thank God she was the one who rescued him. No telling what kind of life he would be living if it wasn't for her."

"Sounds like you're trying to make her out to be some kind of saint. I'm glad she took care of him, but it still doesn't change the fact that he's your kid, Carlton. Our kid. Don't you care about that? Or are you scared your little first lady wife will up and walk out on you, and that mega church you established will throw you out on your face? Is that what's scaring you? You think you're going to lose out on all those millions of dollars that you rake in? You've always been so weak," she said in a spiteful tone.

Carlton prepared to stand up. "I'm not going to sit here and listen to any more of your nonsense. Until you can prove that kid is mine, leave me the hell alone, Breyonna. Go crawl back into the ditch you came from."

Breyonna grabbed hold of Carlton's arm. "I wouldn't be ready to jump up and leave so fast if I were you. I'm not high anymore, Carlton. I'm thinking clear and straight."

"What exactly does that mean?" Carlton asked, rolling his eyes at her and sitting back down in his seat.

"I won't hesitate to tell anyone who'll listen about the secret you and Peyton are hiding. If you want to be sure that Liam is yours, then I'm ready to have a DNA test. You see, when I was using, I admit that I couldn't take care of my kid and love him the way he deserved to be loved. I was too far gone, but you, well you were no saint either. Just because you got your act together doesn't make you better than me. You and Peyton think just because you live here in Adverse City that you have it made. But we'll see about that. Just wait until I talk back to Peyton. She knows I'm serious."

Carlton looked at Breyonna like he could strangle her. His eyes were dark and his mouth was set like he was biting down hard on his bottom lip.

"Are you telling me that Peyton knows you're here in Adverse City?"

"Ha-ha, of course, she knows, stupid. You mean to tell me she hasn't called you up to spill the beans? Hah, umm, I wonder why." Breyonna laughed loudly.

"You shut up your mouth," Carlton ordered, looking around like he was trying to see if there was anyone in the park who might have overheard their conversation. "You think she believes your lie about me being her kid's father? She's no fool. She knows better." Carlton's frown deepened as he got up from the bench and looked down on Breyonna's pencil thin frame.

"Why don't you ask her for yourself. Let her tell you what she believes," Breyonna retorted.

Breyonna was once a gorgeous woman. Her once flowing blonde locks now looked like brittle strands of straw. Her green eyes were set in hollow eye sockets. There was a time she dreamed of being a super model, but all her dreams were dashed when she became an addict.

Breyonna had always been a risk taker. She experimented with pills then cocaine and then on to heroin. She first met Carlton in college. He was messing around real tough with Peyton at the same time, but Breyonna didn't care back then and she didn't care about Peyton now. To her, Peyton was nothing but a spoiled rich kid who treated others like they were beneath her. They ran in the same circles and even called themselves friends, but truth be told, Breyonna never really liked Peyton.

Unlike Peyton, Breyonna was kicked out of college and she returned home to Memphis, strung out and a disappointment to her parents who had worked hard and long hours to send her to college. She looked at herself as a total failure which made her do even more drugs to hide the fact that she had let her parents and herself down.

Breyonna told Carlton that she was pregnant with his kid after one of his pop up visits to Memphis, but of course, he didn't believe her. Why would he when she was nothing more than a drugged out trick. He used her to get him drugs whenever he came to town and a little sex outside of his marriage. He did, however, give her some money after telling her that if she was indeed pregnant that she was in no position to have a kid. He urged her to have an abortion, and she agreed.

Since that incident, Carlton had returned to Memphis once or twice. Like always, he got in touch with Breyonna. He didn't ask about a kid and she didn't mention having one, so he assumed she had gone through with having an abortion or that she was never pregnant in the first place, and if she had been pregnant, it wasn't by him. Whenever he came to Memphis, which wasn't often, all he ever wanted from Breyonna was a chance to chill, get away from his strict family upbringing by smoking a little weed that he laced with cocaine, and of course mess around with Breyonna until it was time for him to return to his all so perfect life in Florida.

Before she resurfaced, Carlton didn't know what had happened to Breyonna or if she was even still alive. He definitely did not know that when Peyton lived in Memphis back in the day that she'd ran into Breyonna. Peyton had never mentioned anything about Breyonna to him and all he knew about Liam, was that she had adopted the kid.

The last time he went to Memphis, which had been years ago, he couldn't find Breyonna to hook up with. He went by the apartment where she used to live and the leasing manager told him that he believed she had been busted for drugs and was locked up. He shrugged it off and on top of it all, he hadn't returned to Memphis since then. Now, here she was, interrupting his life and threatening to destroy everything he had worked hard to achieve. He couldn't let her do that. He had to find a way to make her go away.

"Look, let's stop all of this unnecessary bickering and do right by our kid. It's not too late."

Carlton looked at Breyonna like he was seeing her for the first time. He realized that something wasn't quite right with her. The drugs she'd been on all these years had obviously affected her state of mind because if she thought he was going to be with her she had to be crazy. And if she thought for one minute that he was going to let her pin some illegitimate kid on him, she had to be even crazier.

"Look, you know that's not going to happen. I have a wife and a family of my own. If you love your son like you say you love him then you wouldn't want to disrupt his life. He's a good kid and he has a loving family."

Breyonna popped up from off the bench and positioned herself directly in front of Carlton, almost meeting him eye to eye. "He's our son! And I know you can't be saying that Peyton is better than me. I'm that boy's mother. I did what I thought was best for him at the time."

Carlton tried to reason with her by coming off like he was genuinely concerned and empathetic. "I'm not saying you were a bad mother. You're right. You did what you had to do. But keep in mind, I had no idea you even had a kid, Breyonna."

"Yeah, that's because you're the one who told me to kill him. It's not like you would have won father of the year yourself." Breyonna flailed her arms and started pacing nervously back and forth. "Just because you got money now and you all up in that highfalutin church, preaching to all those uppity, hypocritical, judgmental rich folks, you want to snub your nose at me? If they knew who you really were, I wonder what they would have to say about you then, Carlton. And as far as Peyton goes, what does she have to say about you being that kid's daddy."

Carlton looked like he'd swallowed a bug.

Breyonna suddenly stopped talking and pacing and looked at Carlton. "What's wrong with you? Why are you looking like...hold up." Breyonna stopped in mid-sentence and started laughing and pointing at him. "Ohhh, I see. You two have never talked about it, have you? Well, well, well. Isn't that funny? It's definitely a small world after all. Of all the churches, the cities and towns Peyton could have gone to, she ends up being in

Adverse City and a member of your church, with your kid in tow." She started laughing again. "Talking about something to write about. Now that's a story that needs to be at the top of a bestseller's list."

Carlton's changing complexion signified that she had hit a nerve.

"Look, cut to the chase. How much do you want? If you say it's not money you want, then tell me what it is that you do want. Drugs? Whatever it is, just tell me. And I don't want to hear any more nonsense about me and you getting together. Not going to happen Not back then. Not now. Not ever."

"Let me think on it since I've just been enlightened about these new circumstances. And let me tell you this Carlton Porter, big shot preacher, the stakes just got higher."

■

On his way from meeting with Breyonna, he thought back on the first time he saw Peyton after they had graduated from college and gone on to live separate lives. It was at Perfecting Your Faith that he first saw the boy, too, who was in the arms of Peyton. He had finished his morning sermon and extended the call for those who wanted to join the church, have prayer, or get saved, when Peyton and Derek walked up.

"Peyton?" he said as he shook her hand and then embraced her.

"Yes, it's me." She smiled. "This is my husband, Derek Hudson, and our son, Liam."

"What a pleasant surprise. It's been a long time." Carlton greeted the couple but when he looked at their son, he thought he was seeing things. The boy reminded him so much of Carlton, Jr. Suddenly, he thought about Breyonna and what she'd told him. '*I'm pregnant and it's your kid,'* she had told him. He dismissed the thought, but it didn't stop him from staring at the boy who appeared to be about two years old, the same age as what Breyonna's supposed to be child would be. The boy had the same eyes, the same lost look, the same sandy colored hair as Breyonna. If he did have a kid by Breyonna, he imagined him looking just like this little boy. But Carlton knew that was impossible because this was Peyton and Derek's child. He quickly dismissed all the similarities and welcomed Peyton and her husband to Perfecting Your Faith.

Over the years, Carlton watched as the boy grew up to become a bright, happy kid and now the same little boy was a teenager who Breyonna swore belonged to him and her. As he drove home, Carlton couldn't contain his worry. He called out to God for guidance.

"Father, God. I've messed up. I need you to first of all forgive me for the mistakes of my past. I ask that you work this situation out with Breyonna. I pray that she's lying about Liam and that the truth will be revealed. As for my marriage, Lord, you know I love my wife, but you also know that I'm just not in love with her anymore. My heart belongs somewhere else. I can't stay in this marriage. I just can't."

Chapter 22

"We're just ordinary people." John Legend

Eva chilled on the chaise lounge outside of her home next to the infinity pool. A plum straw beach hat shielded her face from the rays of the sun while her matching bikini barely covered the tiniest portion of skin. On the table next to her was a tall, cold glass of freshly made pineapple mint fruit water. Her headphones were in her ear as she listened to the melodies of John Legend, one of her favorites.

It was the perfect time for her and Harper to sit by the pool together, cuddle, or even make love under the sun. Only Harper, like most mornings, had left for the hospital before the sun made its appearance.

Eva lifted her head up slightly, opened her eyes, and reached for her water. She took a swallow or two of the refreshing drink. Placing it back on the table, she became startled and the glass fell on to the concrete.

"I'm sorry. I didn't mean to scare you," Harper's son said, rushing over to where she was half way sitting up in the lounger. "Don't move. Lemme get something to clean that glass up. I don't want those pretty feet cut up," he said, flashing a smile.

Before one word came out of her mouth, he had disappeared just as quickly as he had appeared. Moments later, he returned with a broom, a dustpan, and portable hand vacuum. He began sweeping the glass into the dustpan and then he started sucking up the remaining glass with the vacuum. Next, he used the broom and dustpan again to gather any remaining glass particles, and one last time followed up by using the handheld vac again.

"I think you got it all," Eva finally said.

"I'm so sorry."

"You didn't do anything. I had my earbuds in and I didn't hear you when you came out here."

"I still should have said something. I didn't mean to intrude on your private time. I thought I'd come out here to swim a few laps. I didn't know you were out here. Where's my dad anyway?"

"Harper usually leaves for the hospital before sunlight, and he doesn't get back home until, well sometimes as late as midnight."

"What a fool." Seth strolled over toward the deep end of the pool.

"Why do you say that about your father?"

"I mean no disrespect to him, but to leave a woman as beautiful as you all alone every day, he has to be nuts."

Eva blushed then looked away.

"You mind?" he said, looking at her, then at the deep blue water.

"No, go ahead."

Seth dove in the pool.

Eva leaned back against the chaise lounge but she still had a good view of Seth. She watched as he swam from one end of the pool to the other, swimming several laps before getting out. Beads of water dripped from his body with the weight of the water tugging on his dark blue swim trunks.

When he met her stare, again she hurriedly focused her gaze on something else.

"You ever get in?" he asked, walking toward her. "Mind if I sit here?" his eyes pointed to the lounger next to hers.

"Of co-orse," she replied. Her accent became more pronounced, something that often happened when she was nervous.

"Of course I can sit here or of course I can't?" He chuckled.

"You can sit there."

"You didn't answer my first question."

"Which was?"

"Do you ever get in the pool?"

"Sure. All the time. I love the water."

"Cool."

Eva sat upright and started getting up. "You stay out here as long as you want. I'm going inside."

"Don't let me run you off."

"You aren't. I usually come out here and meditate, listen to a little music before I start my day. I've done that."

"What kind of music do you like?"

"Hip-hop, R&B, Gospel, Pop. You name it."

"Rap?"

"Yes, of course."

Seth smiled. "I can't see you and my dad sitting around listening to Drake." Seth grinned.

"Your dad is, well, let's just say, the last thing on his mind is music. He's more of a bookworm."

"You don't like reading?"

"No. I mean yes, I enjoy reading, but I was just saying that Harper will choose Time Magazine over music any day." This time Eva laughed lightly as she stood and walked away.

"Owww," she yelped, suddenly stopping and looking down.

"What is it?" Seth asked.

Eva looked at her own blood as it oozed from underneath her foot and on to the concrete.

Seth bounced up and ran toward her. "Man, you're bleeding." He looked briefly around the area where Eva stood. A piece of glass glistened in the sunlight. "Don't

114

move. Glass is still down there. There may be more so hold still."

Seth scooped her up in his muscular arms and carried her inside to the mudroom and sat her down on the all-weather sofa.

"Hold up. Let me get something to clean that cut."

Eva couldn't believe that he had actually picked her up and carried her inside. She wasn't prepared for the rush it gave her. It felt good; like she was a damsel in distress being rescued by prince charming. She smiled then flinched as the stabbing pain at the bottom of her foot brought her back to focus.

Seth used a cloth from the overhead cabinet in the mudroom. He ran cold water on it from the small sink in the room and proceeded to carefully clean the wound and apply pressure to stop it from bleeding. After he finished, he retrieved a band-aid from a first aid kit he saw inside the cabinet too, and put one on the bottom of her foot.

"Come on, let me help you in the house," he offered.

"No, you've done enough. Anyway, it's not bleeding anymore. You put the band-aid on it so I'm good to go."

"You sure?"

"Yeah. I'm good."

Eva got up and walked out of the mudroom with Seth close behind.

When she got close to the stairs, she stopped, almost colliding into him because he was so close up on her.

Out of nowhere, she felt her heart pick up its pace.

"Enjoy your day, Seth."

"Are you sure you're going to be okay? Do you need me to carry you upstairs?"

Eva laughed. "Nooo, really. I'm fine. See you later."

Eva turned away from him and walked upstairs to her room. She hurried up the stairs as quickly as she could considering the bottom of her bandaged foot hurt like she'd cut it with a knife instead of a tiny piece of glass.

Once at the top of the stairs, she turned and looked over her shoulder. Seth was gone. She sucked in a deep breath before slowly releasing it and going to her room to get ready for ladies day out with the girls.

While she dressed, she found herself comparing Harper to his son. They had some similar ways. Harper was charming. It was his charm that swept her off her feet. She found Seth to be the same way, charming that is. Seth shared his father's good looks, dark hair, deep dimples, and dashing smile. Like Harper, he was attentive and caring, only difference was Harper's attention had drifted completely from her to Adverse General.

She smiled to herself when she thought how chivalrous Seth was. It felt good to have someone, particularly a man, to show her some attention.

Eva shook her head as she put on an over the head one-piece colorful dress. The next hour she spent getting dressed then dashed downstairs, out to her car, and drove at lightning speed to meet the housewives.

Chapter 23

"It is easier to forgive an enemy than to forgive a friend." *William Blake*

"Why are you walking like you got something stuck up your behind?" Peyton frowned as Eva approached the table. Peyton was sitting alone, a vodka martini on the table.

"You are so vulgar," Eva told her.

"Call it what you want. Now answer my question. Why are you walking like that?"

"I cut the bottom of my foot on a piece of glass." Eva got ready to pull out her chair when a man walked up behind, beating her to it.

Eva turned around to see who had done such a thoughtful thing. She looked down at the man who was at least two inches shorter than she was. Not only short in stature, he was chubby with a gapped-toothed grin, thick-rimmed glasses but dressed to the nines in what Eva guessed had to have been a tailor made suit. There was no way with his build that he could buy a suit off a rack.

Eva smiled as he held the chair out for her. "Thank you," she said taking a seat.

He answered, "Anytime, my queen," and waddled off while Peyton took a sip of her martini before she started laughing.

"Stop laughing. That was nice of him."

"It sure was," Avery said as she and Meesha walked up to the table and sat down, both ladies smiling.

Right away, the housewives started talking about what had been going during the past week.

Eva talked a little about Seth but she didn't tell the housewives that she felt a weird sort of attraction to him. It wasn't like she couldn't tell them, she just chose not to.

117

There was nothing to tell anyway. Harper was the love of her life. No one would ever be able to take his place.

"Peyton, you need to go to AA," Avery said when the server brought Peyton another martini.

"Don't start with me. Maybe if you had a drink or two sometimes you'd loosen up a bit. Being all uppity and thinking the world revolves around you is not going to cut it, Miss Prissy. At least I'm not trying to kill myself over some foolishness."

"I know you are not trying to come down on me," Avery snapped back. "You think you're all of that? Well, today I'm going to set your lily white behind straight. I'm sick of you always saying something negative. You should be the last one to talk."

"Stop it, ladies," Meesha spoke up. "This is not the time nor the place." Meesha looked around like she was expecting all eyes to be glued to their table.

"She's the one that started it," replied Avery.

"Come on, you two. You heard Meesha," Eva added. "We're supposed to be enjoying ourselves, not sitting here belittling each other.

Peyton rolled her eyes at Avery. "I'm fed up with her, and all of you, for talking about what I do. I'm a grown woman. I don't have to answer to anyone. And back to you, Avery. I've never called you anything other than your name, but you want to call me out of mine? You jealous or something?"

Avery smirked. "Jealous? Are you serious? Why would I be jealous of you, Peyton?"

"I can think of a number of reasons, but I won't even go there. Like Meesha said, this is not the time or the place."

"I think Harper's son has a thing for me," Eva blurted out, like she was hoping her bluntness would produce a much needed break from the mounting tension.

"*Whaaat?* What makes you say that?" Meesha asked.

Avery and Peyton looked at Eva.

"I just know, plus he flirted with me earlier today."

"And?"

"And what?" replied Eva.

"What did you do? What did he do?" Avery asked.

"He didn't do anything and neither did I. You know a woman knows when a man is flirting."

"I guess it makes sense. I mean the two of you are only a few years apart in age. Harper *is* old enough to be your daddy," Peyton stressed.

"See, that's what I mean?" Avery said. "You can never say anything positive. Why don't you sit over there and shut up."

No one seemed to see it coming. Peyton threw the remainder of her vodka martini into Avery's face and within a millimeter of a second, the two women were clawing and scratching at each other.

Eva and Meesha jumped up. Eva grabbed Peyton while Meesha tried to control Avery. Two servers rushed over and helped pull the women apart. One cuss word after another poured from each of their mouths.

Avery used several choice words while Peyton pulled out a few choice words from her vocabulary too.

Once they were separated, the manager came over to their table and asked them to leave. He knew the ladies because they frequented his establishment. He usually made sure they had a table facing the ocean toward the back of the restaurant. There were times they got loud, but they'd never gone as far as they had today.

"I can't believe you two behaved like that. Did you see how everyone was staring at us? And some of those people probably recognize me, too. My Lord, how embarrassing." Meesha folded her arms as the four of them walked outside of the elegant dining establishment. She may not have been the one embroiled in a bitter fight, but she was among them, which made her just as guilty.

As they exited the restaurant and waited outside for the valet attendants to bring their cars around, Eva began speaking in her native tongue. Her lips moved like a speeding freight train with words that were equally as quick.

"Speak English," Avery said. "No one understands that Spanish gibberish."

"I understand every word she's saying. She called us ghetto chicks. But I've got your ghetto chick," Peyton shouted.

"Am I the only one who has some dignity here?" Meesha chimed in. "Look at you two. It's not enough that you acted like fools inside the restaurant, now you're out here still behaving like those hoochies on one of those TV housewives shows. I'm not going to stand here and be embarrassed any longer. I'll talk to you all later." She waved her hand and walked off when she saw the valet attendant driving up in her Bentley.

Hurriedly, Meesha rushed to it, tipped the attendant, got in her car, and sped off without so much as saying another word to her friends.

"Who cares if she left? Who is she supposed to be anyway? Carlton doesn't want her butt either, so she can't talk about me or any of us."

'You're intoxicated. You do not need to drive," Eva told Peyton.

"I am not intoxicated."

"You can't talk sense into someone who refuses to listen," Avery remarked, interrupting Eva's words of caution.

Peyton turned to the side and stared meanly at Avery. "I am not drunk. I can hold my liquor, but even if I couldn't, it's nobody's business." The next valet attendant drove up in Peyton's car, a tan colored Maybach S600, followed by two more Mercedes belonging to Eva and Avery. "You ladies have a good rest of the day. I'm going on to do something fun and exciting." Peyton threw up her hand, walked up to her car, and like Meesha, tipped the driver before getting in her car and speeding away.

"So much for ladies day out," Avery said to Eva. "What are you going to do the rest of the day?"

"Guess I'll go to Aventura Mall. You want to come along?"

"Sure. I'll follow you."

"Okay. Cool."

■

"Meet me in an hour; same place as last time."

"Look, you can't just call and demand that I drop everything I'm doing to come and meet you. I will not be bullied by you." Peyton's anger was easily identifiable as she spoke. Her chest tightened and she sucked in her bottom lip. The drinks she had didn't do anything to keep her calm. A person like Breyonna was the reason she could understand how a person could commit murder. Her life was going good and now this stupid, ignorant dope fiend had showed up and was trying to tear everything apart. Peyton couldn't let that happen. She had to do something or Breyonna would be sure to destroy her family.

"You are the one who chose drugs over your own child, so don't call me up like you've a hopeless victim, because you're not, sweetie."

"One hour. Be there," Breyonna ordered, ending the call without bothering to respond to anything Peyton had said.

Peyton sped toward the restaurant, thinking as she drove that this time she was going to offer Breyonna an amount of money she couldn't refuse. She also wondered if Breyonna had gone to Carlton with her ridiculous claim about Liam being his son. She assumed that she hadn't because Carlton hadn't mentioned anything to her. This made her at ease because that meant that Breyonna had more than likely been lying about Carlton being Liam's biological father. Enough was enough and Peyton was determined to get this settled once and for all so her life could return to normal.

She turned up her nose as she pulled up in the parking lot of the diner. She got out of her car and almost tripped as she stumbled on one of the potholes that laced the small parking area like stepping-stones. She swore underneath her breath.

Opening the door to the diner, she didn't see any sign of Breyonna. She was about to turn and leave. She was not about to play games with some low class, money hungry dope fiend like Breyonna. All she wanted to do was find out what Breyonna's price was to disappear, pay the wench, and say adios forever. Instead, her feet felt glued to the floor, and it wasn't because the floor was dirty and sticky, although it was. It was because the man sitting at the table close to the back window was none other than Carlton.

Peyton's mouth fell open and remained that way. What was he doing here? Had Breyonna really told Carlton the same crap she'd been feeding her about Liam? Peyton cautiously looked around like she was expecting to see Meesha appear, but that would be impossible. She'd just left the housewives and there was no reason for Carlton and Meesha to be at a dump like this.

"What are you doing here?" Carlton asked as he walked up and stood in front of her.

"I should be asking you the same thing, Pastor Porter," Peyton said sarcastically, grimacing. "You screwing some tramp from the other side of the tracks? This is why you want a divorce from my girl?" Peyton accused.

"I see you two have reunited."

Peyton turned quickly toward the sound of Breyonna's voice.

"What are you talking about?" Peyton asked.

"Yeah, what's going on, Breyonna?" Carlton countered.

Peyton needed a drink to calm the butterflies in her tummy. She felt like her head was spinning round and round.

"Have a seat or take your business outside," the grouchy waitress told them.

Breyonna rolled her eyes at the woman. "Chill out, will ya," she said and started walking to a booth at the back of the diner, almost parallel to where Carlton had been sitting.

Peyton and Carlton slowly followed, each one taking a seat in the booth, and both of them sitting next to each other and across from Breyonna.

"Look, I don't know what you're up to, but you better start talking, and you better start talking now," Carlton demanded Breyonna.

Breyonna laughed, her head bobbing backwards like someone had found her tickle spot.

"Look, who do you think you are? Don't come at me like you're in the dark about why I'm here."

"Well, I *am* in the dark," said Peyton, pretending to be shocked that Carlton was at the diner too. "And, Carlton, how long have you known about Breyonna being in Adverse City?" Peyton looked at him as he sat next to her nervously tapping his fingers on the less than clean tabletop.

The same grouchy waitress walked up, chewing gum, and rolling her eyes up in her head. "What are ya having?"

"Nothing for me," Peyton answered abruptly.

"Me neither." Carlton shook his head from side to side.

"Let me have the number six. I want onion rings for my side. Make it a double order and lemonade for my drink," Breyonna said.

The waitress looked back at Peyton then Carlton, rolled her eyes up in her head again, and walked off.

"The least you could have done was order something from the lady. She has to make a living too, you know," Breyonna chastised them.

"If you don't tell me what's going on, and tell me now, I'm leaving," Carlton told her.

"Hey, calm down. You haven't seen your baby momma for a long time," she teased. "Aren't you glad to see me?"

"Cut the crap. Let's get down to business." Peyton snapped.

"Fine by me," Breyonna replied. "It's time for you, *Miss High and Mighty*, to return our son to his parents. Isn't that right, Carlton?"

Chapter 24

"We mistakenly assume that if our partners love us they will react and behave in certain ways - the ways we react and behave when we love someone." John Gray

After being thrown out of the restaurant, Eva tried calling Harper several times but he didn't answer. She decided she would go to the hospital and surprise him.

Stepping off the elevator and on to the second floor, she walked along the shining, pristine looking tiled floors. Out of the corner of her eye, she caught a smile or two from a couple of doctors as she passed by them.

As she neared the nurse's station, she heard her name being called. "Mrs. Stenberg?"

Eva paused and looked at the nurse sitting behind the station. She knew her face but she couldn't recall her name. Quickly she zeroed in on the nurse's nametag.

"Uh, hello, Nicole. How are you?"

"I'm good. It's been a long time since I've seen you," she slightly stammered.

The nurse sitting next to her stared at Eva, and mumbled, "Hello," and then looked away.

"Dr. Stenberg is in surgery," Nicole explained. "Is he expecting you?"

"No, not really. I was out this way," Eva lied, "so I thought I'd surprise him." Eva smiled.

"I'm not sure when he'll be done."

"It's no problem; I'll wait." Eva turned to walk away, then stopped and looked back over her shoulder at Nicole. "Will you let me in his office?" she stated, not really asking but more like telling.

"I..."

The nurse sitting next to her mumbled something to Nicole.

"Is there a problem?" Eva walked back to the nurses' station.

"It's just that Dr. Stenberg doesn't allow anyone to wait in his office, unless..."

"Unless what?" Eva said, placing one hand on her hip, while giving both nurses the evil eye.

"Unless he's told us that he's expecting someone," the other nurse said. "Me, personally, I don't want to get in trouble." She looked at Nicole. "It's your call."

"I promise you, my husband will not have a problem with me waiting on him in his office. Now, please, come and unlock the door or give me the key and I'll let myself in."

Nicole reluctantly stood, walked from behind the nurses' station, and headed to Harper's office around the corner and at the end of the hallway where the staff offices were located.

"Thank you, Nicole," Eva told her when the woman unlocked the door, opened it, and flicked the light switch on.

"You're welcome. Like I said, I don't know how long it will be before he returns."

"I know. I'm patient."

Nicole nodded and walked off.

Eva looked around Harper's office. It was immaculate. Everything was in its proper place. Harper was methodical like that at home, too. Everything had to be in order and just the way he liked it. T-shirts color coded, folded, and on the shelf together; white dress shirts, starched and hanging on the hangers together. Colored socks in one drawer; white socks in another. It had taken Eva some getting used to when they first got married, but Harper was good about it. He seemed to understand that she was not used to his OCD lifestyle and so he tried to make things easy for her. Before they got married, he had a full time housekeeper. He asked Eva if she wanted to keep Marissa on as the housekeeper, and Eva readily told him that she did. There was no way she could maintain the house in the perfect order that Harper liked.

Marissa, an older Hispanic woman, who didn't speak English very well, was nice and accepting of Eva. She took the time to show her how Harper liked things, taught her about the kinds of foods he liked, the way he liked his laundry folded, and his bed made. When it was just the two of them, they spoke in their native tongue which seemed to please Marissa.

Eva thumbed through a copy of *The New Yorker* sitting on a square table that had a magazine compartment underneath. Smiling, she ran her fingertips along Harper's oak desk as she studied the pictures he had of the two of them on their wedding day. Another picture showed them on their honeymoon posed in front of the pink Lake Hillier in Australia. It was the honeymoon of a lifetime. But as beautiful as that time was, it quickly disappeared when they returned to the states. When Harper was appointed as chief cardiologist and medical director, Eva turned into a lonely, childless young bride starving for her husband's love, attention, and affection.

When she met Avery and Ryker at a fundraising dinner party for one of Harper's friends who was running for a seat on the senate, it was a welcome relief. She and Avery hit it off, and soon after, Avery introduced her to Peyton and Meesha. Meesha invited her and Harper to attend Perfecting Your Faith. Harper readily accepted the invitation when Eva came home after enjoying her first ladies day out with the housewives and told him about it.

Harper told Eva that he had heard great things about the church and the church's pastor, Carlton Porter. Sunday, one of the few days Harper was at home, unless called for an emergency was Eva's favorite day of the week. It meant having some alone time with her man. They visited Perfecting Your Faith several times and on the drive home after church one afternoon, Harper told her that he wanted them to become members of the church.

Eva was happy to hear Harper's decision about Perfecting Your Faith. The church they formerly attended was small and the members acted cold and indifferent toward her. She didn't know if it was because they were an interracial couple or not, but whatever their reason, Eva did not feel comfortable. Perfecting Your Faith was different. People didn't seem to care about race or ethnicity. The church was quite diverse, and it was not unusual at all to see interracial couples, black, white, Hispanic men, women, and children. Eva felt as if she fit right in. Meeting the housewives added to her feeling of acceptance.

Harper, Carlton, Derek, and Ryker became friends, too, not close friends like the housewives, but on those occasions that one of the housewives entertained, the men were sure to attend, if at all possible.

She picked up the picture and fought back the urge to cry. She wanted to have Harper's baby so badly. Why couldn't he understand that a baby would bring them closer together? A baby would bring so much happiness to her life; she wouldn't be so lonely. But Harper, no matter how she begged and pleaded, put her off. It was selfish of him, the housewives told her, and she was beginning to agree with them.

Behind his desk was another table, an oblong one that looked more like a sofa table. It had several more pictures, which were mostly pictures of Seth taken during key moments in his life. One was of him graduating from kindergarten, another of him with his pee wee soccer team, then another when he graduated from high school, and a more recent one with him standing on the steps in front of what Eva assumed was his mother's house.

Eva blushed as she replayed the image of him wet and in his swim trunks. He was sexy and fine just like his daddy.

"How long have you been here?'

Eva jumped slightly, startled at hearing Harper's baritone voice as he entered his office.

"Not too long." She walked over to Harper, placed both arms around his neck, stood on her tiptoes, and kissed him.

She could feel his body tense up as he gently pushed her away.

"Aren't you happy to see me?" She tried kissing him again, and again he pushed her away, walked to his desk, pulled out his chair, and sat down.

"I've been in surgery for the past six hours. I'm tired. The last thing I expected was for my wife to be in my office waiting on me like you're trying to catch me doing something other than what I do."

"Catch you? What are you talking about? I'm not trying to catch you doing anything. I wanted to surprise you." Eva's voice revealed her hurt and disappointment. "I thought you would be glad to see me. Most nights I'm asleep when you get home and you leave before I wake up. *Te echo de menos*, Harper," Eva said in her native tongue. She approached him cautiously this time. She stood behind him and began to massage his temples.

"I'm sorry. I just wasn't expecting you."

"I know." She continued to massage his temples, and then slowly moved to his shoulders. Eva felt him start to relax.

She kissed the top of his head as she continued to massage him.

"Ahh, that feels good. I wish I could sit here all day, but I can't. I still have rounds to make. I'm sorry," he apologized.

Eva's hands dropped to her side as she moved from behind him. Harper stood up and kissed her on her forehead.

"Why don't you go on home, while I finish up here? I promise I'll try to make it home early tonight. Okay?"

Eva feigned a smile. "Sure." Quickly, she walked over to the table where she'd placed her purse, picked it up, and walked to the door.

"Eva, wait."

"What?"

He walked up to her, took her by the waist, and pulled her to him. He kissed her with passion until her body ached for his touch. He caressed her hips and his hands explored her inner thighs. Pushing the door closed with his foot, he sandwiched her between himself and the door.

Eva released a moan of satisfaction. "I want you so bad," she whispered as she explored his body as expertly as he explored hers.

He was silent, but his kisses were fiery and hot.

Reaching down for his most prized possession, she stopped suddenly, pushed him away, and glared at him. From the feel of things, Harper was not excited in the least. He didn't want her; he was only trying to pacify her.

"What? What's wrong?"

"What's wrong?" She threw her head back and chuckled. "What's wrong? Absolutely nothing. That's what's wrong!" Eva opened the door and stormed out.

Chapter 25

"You don't destroy people you love." Unknown

Eva ran inside the house. Her hot tears poured down her face as she rushed up the steps. Blinded by hurt and tears, she didn't see Seth bolting down the stairs. The two collided. Had it not been for his steady hand grabbing hold of her petite waist she would have fallen down the stairs. Instead, she fell on the landing with him practically on top of her.

"Whoa," he said. "You almost became a statistic," he chuckled as their bodies touched.

The tears didn't stop. Just the opposite happened. She sobbed uncontrollably.

Seth eased off of her, took hold of her hand, and with much ease he helped her to her feet. "What's wrong?

Eva bowed her head but not before seeing the look of sincerity shining through his mocha colored eyes. His eyes were so striking that they looked like they were fake, like he wore contacts; but he did not. It was all him.

"I'm sorry," she said as she broke free of his grip, and took off running up the rest of the stairs to her bedroom. She closed the door behind her and fell across her bed.

Moments later, she heard a light knock. She slowly sat up and listened to the knocking sound again.

"Eva, you all right in there?" she heard Seth ask.

Why wouldn't he leave her alone? Couldn't he see that she was upset and didn't want to be bothered? She decided not to answer him, hoping that he would give up and go away.

Knock. Knock.

Shelia E. Bell

Eva remained quiet, lying back on the bed again. She heard Seth as he walked away from her door. It wasn't long after before she fell asleep.

Meesha sat with the kids in the family room as they watched a popular kid's movie for what was probably the third or fourth time. She picked up her cell phone and texted Carlton - again. Usually he would come home from church early afternoon, leave for an hour or so to go back to church and be back home for the evening by five thirty, unless he had an evening service or a speaking engagement somewhere. Even then, he would come home, eat dinner with the kids, and maybe take a power nap before returning to church. But it was already past six and she hadn't heard anything from him. It was so unlike him not to call or come and check on them, and for him not to respond to any of the four text messages she had sent previously had her concerned. Maybe he was with her, the other woman. *Does she have kids? Does she make love better than me? Is she prettier than me?* A million questions filtered through her mind. Carlton told her that another woman was not the reason he wanted a divorce, but from the way things were looking, Meesha wasn't buying it.

Ding. The sound of her text message jarred her from her thoughts.

"n a meeting. b there soon as I can."

Meesha rolled her eyes as she threw her phone down on the couch next to her. She got up from the sofa, leaving the kids to watch the last half hour of the movie without her. In the kitchen, she stood at the island and allowed her tears to flow freely out of sight and away from the boys. Life for her had changed in a flash.

The Real Housewives of Adverse City

"God, what is this?" she cried out as she looked up toward the ceiling. "Why is this happening and what am I supposed to do?"

For the next several minutes, she remained in the kitchen struggling to regain her composure. She didn't want the boys to see her upset; and she definitely didn't want them to see her crying. Why couldn't Carlton see what he was doing to his family? Did he even care anymore?

"Father God, I need you. I can't make it through this. If this is a test, help me to see it and help me to pass it."

Meesha tore off a paper towel, wiped her face, dried her tears, and returned to the family room. Sitting back down on the couch, she told the boys to come and sit next to her. They did as they were told, and she stretched her arms across the length of her sons in an embrace, viewing the rest of the movie with them in silence. Her mind raced in a thousand different directions. Who was this other woman that had captured the heart of the man she loved with all of her heart? Carlton had been her king and she had been his queen for a very long time, with Meesha never having had reason to doubt his loyalty and faithfulness to her and their marriage—until now.

Meesha continued to allow her thoughts to run awry. Carlton may have wanted out but she would have to show him that it wasn't going to be so easy to up and walk away from her. She had been playing the role of submissive wife long enough. If he thought that she was going to roll over and let him walk all over her, he had another thing coming. It was time she showed him how a *real* housewife plays the game.

Chapter 26

"Some people are like clouds; when they disappear it's a brighter day." Unknown

Carlton decided that this next meeting with Breyonna would be his final meeting and it needed to take place in a private space.

Carlton and Meesha owned two residential properties that they leased. The young couple who had been leasing one of the houses for the past two years recently relocated, so it was the perfect place to meet up with Breyonna and Peyton.

Peyton drove up behind Carlton as he turned into the driveway of the rental home. Breyonna followed in an old black and red, beat up Chevy Malibu driven by a bearded, unkempt, crackhead looking fellow.

Carlton pushed his remote and the garage door opened. He drove in, pushed the button to close it and then quickly got out of his car, walked up to the front door of the house and unlocked it. He entered the house and headed straight to the side door to direct the women inside.

"By yourself," he said forcefully to Breyonna when he saw the driver's door open and the guy got out.

"He's not coming in," she said roughly. The guy leaned against the car, reached inside his shirt pocket, and pulled out a pack of cigarettes and a lighter.

Breyonna walked around the car and up toward the house. As she stepped inside, she looked around like she had just walked inside a million dollar mansion instead of a modest hundred thousand dollar home.

"I must say, you have done quite well for yourself, Carlton," Breyonna begrudgingly complimented.

"I don't need your shallow compliments," Carlton snapped. "We're here for business, to settle this mess you're trying to stir up once and for all."

"Boy, please, I'm not the one stirring up mess. You and her are to blame for all of this. All y'all had to do was let me see my kid."

Peyton walked up on Breyonna. "Listen to me, if you think you're going to waltz your little behind here in Adverse City and steal my son, you have another thing coming." Peyton was furious. She definitely could use a stiff drink. Carlton eyed her like he could read her mind but he didn't move.

Breyonna laughed. "First, let me set the record straight - he is *not* your kid. Second, I suggest you get up outta my face or I won't be responsible for what happens next."

"Look, let's not do this. We're here for business, not for one of your gutter fights," Carlton told Breyonna, as he frowned. "Peyton is the only mother Liam knows, and I know you aren't so heartless that you would destroy his future because of your selfish motives. If it's money you need, I told you before to tell me how much, and I'll see what I can do to tide you over until you catch a break. I have some contacts where you live who I can reach out to, maybe help you get a job."

"Hah, you think it's going to be that easy? You think you can just pay me off and I'll go away, just like that?" Breyonna popped her fingers, plopped down in a nearby chair, and laughed.

Peyton frowned, folded her arms, and rolled her eyes up in her head. "You are nothing but a scamming, scheming, skank!"

Breyonna kept laughing. "Oh, so it's come to name calling now, huh? You Christian folk kill me. You're so fake. And Carlton, a man of God? Honey, please. You want to believe that you know Carlton so well. You didn't know him back then and you don't know him now. Then again, hey, maybe you've changed." Breyonna looked at Carlton who looked like the color had been drained from his body.

Carlton swallowed deeply. He always felt that one day his past would catch up to him but every time he prayed, he hoped that today wouldn't be that day. He always used to hear his father talking about this being a small world we lived in. As a kid, he never quite understood what his father was talking about. Now he knew.

"Listen, and listen to me good. This is the last time I'm going to say this. You are nothing to Liam, Peyton. You have no rights to him whatsoever. You'll be lucky if your behind don't go to prison. I have a mind to let the police know that you kidnapped my boy. Then we'll see who has the last laugh." Next, she focused on Carlton and said, "No more secrets. It's time to introduce our son to his real parents."

Chapter 27

"It takes a fool to learn that love don't love nobody."
The Spinners

Avery and Eva texted back and forth for over an hour before Avery ignored Eva's last text and called her on the phone instead. The conversation at hand had become too intense and it would take too much time for Avery to tell Eva everything she had to say. Hearing Eva admit that she was attracted to her stepson was reason for concern to Avery. If Eva crossed the line with Seth, her marriage would be over.

Avery heard the desperation in Eva's voice when she called.

"What's wrong with watching a movie and sharing a meal with him? There's plenty of food and no one to eat it. I don't see the harm in that," explained Eva.

"Girl, don't play. It's me you're talking to. You are not going to tell me that Seth invited you to the guest house just to watch a movie and eat a sandwich. He's no kid and neither are you. Do not put yourself in a position where you can be tempted to do something you might regret later."

Eva released a heavy sigh. "But I'm bored. I'm tired of sitting in this house alone every day.

"What happened to joining the Women's Outreach Ministry? You said you wanted to become more involved with church activities and from what Meesha says, the outreach ministry is really active. They go to some of the less fortunate areas and perform community service. They do a lot of activities with single moms and their kids. And as much as you love children, it could be a good outlet for you."

Eva sighed and paced a few steps across the hardwoods. "I forgot all about that. Maybe I'll check it out the next time they have a meeting. But you know what I really want?"

"Need I ask?"

"I want my own baby. That would make me so happy."

Silence infiltrated the phone for a fraction of a second before Avery responded. "Look," she said then hesitated again.

"What?" said Eva.

"Uhhh, who says you can't have Harper's kid?"

"What are you talking about?"

"What I'm saying is, what would he do if you were to get pregnant anyway? I mean, he'll probably be pissed for a while, but hey, he'll get over it."

Eva stopped pacing, and stood completely still in the center of the family room. "But how?"

"What do you mean *how*? It hasn't been that long for you has it?" Avery snickered over the phone.

"I mean, it's not like we make love every night. When Harper gets home, he's usually tired. All he wants to do is eat a little something, take a shower, and go to bed and most of the time that doesn't include making love to me," Eva complained. "We have sex maybe once every couple of weeks. I'm telling you, Avery, I don't know how much longer I can take this."

"Listen to me. I hate that I'm suggesting you do this, but sometimes we have to take matters into our own hands."

"What are you suggesting?"

"You want a baby. Right?"

"Right?"

"And you're the one who's going to be taking care of the child, right?"

"Of course."

"Then I suggest you start making plans to pick out your nursery."

"I don't follow you," Eva replied, sounding confused.

"Do not take another birth control pill. You follow me now?"

Eva paused before answering. She couldn't believe Avery was suggesting that she deceive her husband. But the more she thought about it, the more her upside down smile turned upright. Avery was right. Harper would be mad but she was sure that once he saw the beautiful child they made together, his feelings would change.

"I follow you. But weren't you the one who said I should respect what Harper wants and be patient, and things would change?"

"That was then; this is now. Now it's time you take matters into your own hands."

Eva paused a second or two before saying, "I'm going to do it. No more pills. Operation make-a-baby is in effect." Eva smiled, relishing the thought of getting pregnant and having a baby by the man she loved.

"And don't say a word to Harper, not to anyone, that includes Peyton and Meesha. All you need is for Peyton to have one too many vodka tonics and she'll tell all of your secrets. And Meesha, well you already know that she will quote every scripture or Bible passage she can find to convince you that what you're doing is wrong. But it's not wrong. You're married to this man. You want a child. Some women take birth control pills faithfully and still wind up pregnant. You can be one of them."

"You're right."

"Time will tell just how fertile you are," added Avery. "So feed him when he comes home tonight and after that no matter how much he complains about being tired, you know what you have to do."

Shelia E. Bell

"Yes. I know." Eva started laughing almost hysterically over the phone. "Thank you. Thank you so much."

"We housewives have to stick together. Look, I'll talk to you tomorrow. It's time for me to go pick up the girls."

"And it's almost time for me to take my girls to the spa."

"Yeah, you have got to get pregnant, and real soon. Those three pups you call your girls are too spoiled. I can only imagine how you're going to spoil your kid."

"I love my babies." As soon as she said it, the three canines came bolting into the family room followed by the dog walker."

"They've had their walk, Mrs. Stenberg. Is there anything else you need before I leave?" the dog walker slash college freshman asked Eva.

"No, that's it. Hold on just a sec please," she told the young girl. "I'll talk to you later, Avery. And thanks again."

"No problem. Buh-bye."

Eva ended the call and then focused her attention back on the young lady. "Let me get your money. I'll be right back." Eva turned to go retrieve the money from her bedroom, came back, and paid the girl.

When the young lady left, Eva sprawled out on the chaise sofa to think about what Avery said. When the three pooches jumped up on the sofa, snuggling next to her, she smiled as she thought about the child she would soon be holding in her arms. Her thoughts took her captive so much so that she dozed off. Less than an hour later, after the dogs woke her up with their constant barking, she got up, checked the time, and then loaded them in their kennels so she could take them to their monthly overnight grooming and spa session. She loved her Yorkies like a mother loved her kids. That's one of

140

the reasons she knew she would make a good mother. If she could be patient, attentive, and loving to her pooches, she knew her love would be unmeasurable toward a child of her own.

■

Eva headed home after dropping the dogs off at the groomer. At the traffic light, she glanced over and saw The Bake Shop, one of Harper's favorite places to get sweets. She wasn't gung-ho on eating a lot of sweets, but it was Harper's weakness. Being a cardiologist, he tried to take care of himself, but sweets from The Bake Shop was one of the loves of his life, and he indulged in the delectable delights every now and then.

When the light changed to green, Avery glanced slightly over her shoulder to see if there was a car in her blind spot before she put on her left turn signal, got over in the turn lane, and headed to The Bake Shop. Once inside, she studied the rows of beautifully decorated goodies. She decided on a dozen assorted cupcakes for her hubby and Seth to share because somewhat like his father, Seth loved to indulge in sweets, too.

Next, she voice dialed Déjà Vu Restaurant and placed an order for another one of Harper's favorite dishes which consisted of grilled tilapia topped with a creamy reduction of fresh lump crabmeat, crawfish and shrimp. She ordered collard greens and roasted garlic potatoes for his sides. For herself, she decided she would prepare a nice side spinach and broccoli salad when she got home. That wouldn't take too long. She reasoned she could easily get home, chill for an hour or so, and think of the fun it was going to be seducing her husband.

While waiting on her food order, Eva took a seat at the always busy restaurant, and again allowed her mind to think about the colors she would decorate her baby's nursery. The bedroom at the far end of the hall was the room she decided would be the nursery. The more she thought about it, the more excited she became. For the first time in months, she actually felt happy.

Eva thought about calling her mother who still lived in Bolivia, to ask her advice about Harper, but she decided against it. Her mother wasn't thrilled that Eva had married him because, in her eyes, he was too old for her daughter. Her father remained neutral when it came to the decisions his children made. She would take Avery's advice and keep her plan of deception to herself.

■

Avery filed in behind the long, slow moving line of cars as they winded around and through the driveway leading up to the front of the girls' school. She thought about the advice she'd given Eva. "Forgive me. I shouldn't have encouraged my friend to deceive Harper. But she wants a child so badly. And I know she'll love it with all of her soul," Avery prayed aloud.

Praying was not something she made a habit of doing, but she could feel her thought process gradually taking on a spiritual like transformation. She had never been the overly religious type, and hadn't grown up in the church like Meesha. Her family life was just the opposite. Her mother was a self-proclaimed atheist and weird as it may sound, her father was a Jehovah's Witness. How unbelievably crazy was that. Imagine the household she grew up in. There was constant fighting and warring over what Avery and her brother were going to be brought up to believe or not believe. Turns out that Avery pretty much shared her father's beliefs while her brother leaned more toward the nonbelief of their mother. *I should call and tell her not to do it,* Avery thought. Then again, she had secrets, too. Secrets that could tear apart her life and the life of the man she desperately loved.

Heather and Lexie were each led to the car by their teachers as Avery steered into the circular drive of the school pick-up area. Once inside, the girls were full of chatter about all the activities they had participated in at school that day. Both of them were involved in instrumental and choral music, ballet, and foreign languages. Lexie played violin and loved it. Heather was more excited about learning to speak Chinese and Spanish, which she was actually becoming really good at.

Listening to her girls made Avery thankful more each day that God had spared her life. The thought of Heather and Lexie growing up without her was something she did not want to think about. She had learned from her near death experience that life was too precious. She was determined to not let anything ruin her life and deprive her from living anymore, including Ryker. Her future was bright and she would soon be with the one she loved *and* who loved her.

Chapter 28

"One of a kind love affair it is." Unknown

It had been two weeks since Peyton had talked to
Breyonna or Carlton. She hadn't gone to church for the
past couple of Sundays either, afraid that Breyonna might
show up there and cause a scene.

Today, she pushed her reservations aside and drove to
Perfecting Your Faith, after calling and texting Carlton
for the past week, and not getting the type of response she
felt she deserved, she decided it was time to talk to him
face to face. Also, she didn't like the idea of leaving a
trail of phone calls for Meesha to stumble upon. Meesha
didn't seem like the type who would go through Carlton's
phone searching for trouble, but Peyton didn't want
Meesha to learn about any of this until the time was right.

Peyton approached the receptionist counter. The
name plate on the desk was "ZELMA FENTRESS,
RECEPTIONIST." Peyton told the receptionist that she
needed to see Carlton Porter, that it was a personal matter
of importance. Like all good gatekeepers, Mrs. Fentress
advised Peyton that she would have to make an
appointment through Carlton's personal administrative
assistant.

Peyton explained further that she needed to see the
pastor right away. Again, Mrs. Fentress refused Peyton.

Peyton did not want to lose her cool. She inhaled,
pursed her lips, and calmly tried convincing the older
woman that she didn't need an appointment and all Mrs.
Fentress needed to do was call the pastor and tell him she
was there.

Mrs. Fentress continued insisting that Peyton make an

appointment. Peyton started tapping her long polished nails on the top of the smooth surfaced counter.

"Look, you don't understand. This is an urgent matter. I need to speak to Carl...I mean to Pastor Porter immediately. Please, just call him."

Peyton didn't know if it was divine intervention or what, but she looked up when she heard Carlton's booming voice.

"Remember, I want to see you at church Sunday," Carlton said to the well-dressed woman walking along next to him.

"I plan to be here. You just don't know, these counseling sessions have made a huge difference in my life," the woman said.

"To God be the glory," Carlton responded.

Peyton looked around, following the sound of familiar voices.

"Avery?" Peyton said in a surprised tone when she saw Avery and Carlton appear from around the corner.

"Good day, Sister Hudson," Carlton spoke to Peyton.

"Hello, Pastor. You're just the man I need to see." Peyton looked briefly at Mrs. Fentress and rolled her eyes.

"What are you doing here?" Avery asked, stopping the exchange.

"I could ask you the same thing."

Avery glanced back at Carlton and then looked at the nosy receptionist who was watching and listening like she was tuned in to a soap opera.

"Pastor Porter has been my spiritual counselor since, well, since you know..." Avery leaned in and said softly, "since I got out of the hospital."

"Oh, I didn't know," Peyton whispered back. "You never told me, or any of the housewives, at least I don't *guess* you told the others." Peyton stepped back and looked peeved.

Avery didn't bother addressing Peyton's remark. "What are you doing here?" she asked instead.

"I can use some spiritual counseling of my own," Peyton answered.

"Um, is that right? Well, I can tell you that Pastor has helped me understand a lot about God's love and self-forgiveness." Avery smiled and looked at Carlton who nodded and returned her smile.

"That's good, Avery," Peyton said.

"Well, look, I've got to get out of here. I have some errands to run. We'll talk later. Thank you again, Pastor."

"You're welcome and God bless you, Sister Avery," Carlton said in return, placing his hand on the center of her back as he guided her toward the exit and held the door open for her.

Avery walked off, strolling confidently away in a striking Stella McCartney pantsuit.

Carlton turned and walked away from the door. "How can I help you, Sister Hudson?" Carlton asked Peyton as he took a quick glance over his shoulder in time to see Avery open the door to her car and get inside.

Mrs. Fentress spoke up. "Pastor Porter, I tried to tell her that she would need to schedule an appointment, but she refused." The receptionist cut her eyes at Peyton.

"It's okay, Mrs. Fentress. I'll see her. My next appointment isn't set to arrive until much later." He walked up to the counter.

"Yes, Pastor Porter. No problem."

Mrs. Fentress, looking perturbed, rolled her eyes at Peyton all while smiling as she responded to Pastor Porter. She knew exactly who Peyton Hudson was. She, along with the one who'd just left was one of the three women who were good friends with the First Lady. They were rich and uppity and all of them, except the first lady, acted like the sun rose and set on their behinds.

Mrs. Fentress and some of the other senior citizen church women would often gossip about how the housewives paraded in the church Sunday after Sunday in their fancy heels, wearing their expensive garb, and carrying their designer handbags.

"Thank you for seeing me, Pastor Porter. I promise I won't take up much of your time," she told Carlton as she strolled confidently pass the receptionist counter and toward Carlton without acknowledging Mrs. Fentress.

"Mrs. Fentress, please see if the small conference room down the hall is available. No need to go all the way back to my office," he said, looking at Peyton.

"Sure. Give me a few minutes," Mrs. Fentress replied.

"How are you?" Pastor Porter stated, trying to sound like he wasn't worried about what he felt Peyton had come to see him about. He hadn't heard from nor seen Breyonna since their last encounter, and she refused to leave information on how to get in touch with her. He prayed that her disappearance meant she had decided to leave things as they were.

Carlton tried to think of ways that he could tell Meesha about Liam, but the more he thought about it, the more he realized there was no easy way. Once she found out that he had a son, and that son was Peyton's kid, then she would be the one running to divorce court. The fact that he had a mistress was bad enough, but this situation right here? And the media? The media would have a field day and his ministry could go to ruins.

Carlton had to find a way to keep Breyonna from divulging his dirty laundry. The news about him and Meesha getting a divorce would be out soon enough. That, coupled with the possibility of Peyton's kid being his, and his life could be ripped apart. He didn't want

147

things to blow up any sooner than he knew they were about to. He was sorry for some of the things he'd done in his past. Unearthing them could not only affect his life now, but he could only imagine what it would do to a youngster like Liam. It had been a blessing for Carlton to watch the boy grow up and become a responsible, kind, and smart young man who had a lot going for himself.

"So how long have you been counseling her?"

"You know I can't discuss that."

"Dang, Carlton. It's no secret that she tried to kill herself, so I assume that it's at least been since then, huh?"

"Look, let's not talk about Avery. Have you heard from Breyonna?"

Peyton trembled as she sat at the middle section of the oblong oak table across from Carlton. "No, and that's why I'm here. I have a weird feeling that she's up to something, and it can't be good." She waited on Carlton's response, hoping he could tell her that he had somehow convinced Breyonna to leave well enough alone.

Carlton shook his head, glancing up from time to time at the closed conference room door as if he expected Breyonna to burst inside any minute. "I haven't heard from her either. That worries me."

"You know her better than I do. What do you think is going on with her? I mean, she won't accept our offers of money, and she says she won't leave Adverse City without seeing Liam. She goes from threatening us to not hearing from her at all."

"Breyonna was the kind of girl who was after any guy who she thought could offer her a privileged life. In the end, she let drugs get the best of her. And you and her, well, I never told you, but that hurt me, Carlton. That hurt me really bad," Peyton confessed. A sad countenance filled her face.

Carlton shifted his eyes from Peyton. He rested his head in his hands for a couple of seconds. "I was sorry back then and I'm sorry now."

His words sounded so sincere and for the first time in all these years, Peyton felt like she could forget about Carlton's betrayal of the love she thought they once shared.

"I used to think she was cool because while you were serious most of the time, Breyonna liked to party. Me, I was serious about my studies, but I liked to party then, too." Carlton sighed deeply. "You know the history. No need to go down that road again."

"I hope you aren't trying to slick blame *me* for *your* screw up," Peyton retorted.

Carlton raised both hands in surrender. "Please, just let it go. After all these years, you still haven't forgiven me. But there's nothing I can do about it now, Peyton. All of that's in the past."

"If it was all in the past it wouldn't be affecting us today, now would it? The past is what's trying to ruin both of our lives, Carlton! And my marriage is already on shaky ground. Breyonna was always jealous of me and of our relationship back then. And to this day, I do not know why." Peyton started crying. "Why did she have to come here? If she cared about Liam, she would leave Adverse City and never come back."

Carlton reached out and laid his hand on top of Peyton's. "Don't cry. Please don't cry." He looked up and around again toward the door. "We're going to figure this out. If we know one thing about Breyonna, she may say she doesn't want money, but we both know that she can be bought. We just have to find her price."

"I don't feel like that anymore, because if she wanted money so badly, then why wouldn't she accept our offers? What are we going to do?" Peyton almost sounded hysterical as her voice rose and her eyes flooded with tears. Her hands trembled underneath Carlton's hand.

"What we have to do is keep our cool. I'm praying for direction. I'm standing on God's word. First Corinthians ten and thirteen says, no temptation has overtaken you that is not common to man. God is faithful, and he will not let you be tempted beyond your ability, but with the temptation he will also provide the way of escape, that you may be able to endure it."

"That sounds good, Carlton. Sounds real good, but it doesn't make me feel any better. I'm scared and to tell you the truth, I don't feel good about not hearing from her. We have to do something."

"Look, I'll try to find her. I promise."

"She's been planning this for a while," Peyton said.

Peyton questioned her sensibility. How could she have taken another woman's child without pressing Breyonna to give her legal guardianship? What was she thinking back then? Then again, she quickly reminded herself that Breyonna didn't want the boy; didn't want anything but her next high. Now here it was, years later and this woman was in Adverse City for payback. And if she didn't get what she wanted, like a tornado, Breyonna was ready to destroy everyone in her path.

Carlton got up and walked around to where Peyton was sitting. He reached down and took hold of her hand and tugged on it slightly until she stood up. Putting his arm around her shoulders, he pulled her into his chest. She leaned in and allowed her tears to fall upon his suit coat and her head to rest against him.

The knock on the door startled them. Peyton's head popped up. She hastily wiped the tears from her eyes as Carlton pushed a chair out of his way and pounced toward the door.

The Real Housewives of Adverse City

"Yes, what is it?" he asked when he opened the door and saw his administrative assistant, Jeanine, standing on the other side.

Jeanine's doe-shaped eyes wandered past him as she stole a look at Peyton. It wasn't often that he used the small conference room near the side entrance of the church. It was usually reserved for small meetings held by the staff, so she was curious when Mrs. Fentress told her about Peyton Hudson's sudden appearance. Something wasn't right. Not only had Peyton popped up without an appointment to see the pastor, now there was another woman insisting on seeing him, too. This woman was in stark contrast to the fabulosity of Peyton.

Jeanine didn't recall ever seeing the woman before, but with an active membership of over 20,000, there was no way she knew every single person that walked through the church doors insisting on seeing the pastor. They did it all the time; many with agendas that included trying to seduce the pastor in any way that they could. They would come waltzing in the church during the week with all sorts of excuses and reasons for needing to see him. Jeanine and Mrs. Fentress, too, could practically smell whether they were in real need of pastoral counseling or if they were there to entice Pastor Carlton into something ungodly.

Rumor had it that he had asked the first lady for a divorce, but Jeanine didn't believe it. She was privy to much confidential information and overheard many a surprising conversation between the pastor and his trusted deacons. There were times she overhead him counseling some of the church members, too. Their complaints ranged from troubled children to incest among family members to dealing with sexual identity and criminal acts. There was practically no subject that she hadn't

151

heard mentioned, but she kept it all confidential. Well, at least most of it.

"I'm sorry to disturb you, Pastor Porter, but there's someone who insists on seeing you," Jeanine whispered. "I told her you were unavailable and tried to get her to make an appointment."

"Have Minister Davis or one of the other ministers on call to see her. I'm in an important meeting right now. So please, do not disturb me again." He didn't want to come off sounding irritated with Jeanine, but how many times did he have to remind her that they had a full staff of ministers who were trained counselors. It was their job to listen and provide assistance to the church. No one man could possibly do it all.

"Yes, Pastor Porter. I'm sorry."

Jeanine glimpsed over her shoulder as Pastor Porter closed the door. Whatever he and Peyton Hudson were talking about seemed serious. Jeanine could tell from the look on Pastor Porter's face. His eyeballs bulged like someone who had thyroid problems and though it was an otherwise cool and calm fall day, beads of sweat clung to the pastor's head.

From what Jeanine could see of Peyton Hudson, she looked flustered too. Was Peyton the reason for the rumors about Pastor and the first lady's troubled marriage? She shook her head briefly as the illicit thought played out in her mind. Pastor Porter was a man true enough, but the Pastor Porter she had come to love and respect was no adulterer…at least she hoped he wasn't.

"I can't believe that you never told me you were Liam's father. And you were going to Memphis sleeping with her and from what she says, you and her would get high together, too? Oh, my God, Carlton, what were you thinking? Was getting high and screwing someone like Breyonna worth it? Look at what you've gotten yourself into...and me. I thought it was another one of Breyonna's lies when she first told me all those years ago that you were Liam's daddy. How could you watch him grow up practically before your eyes, and not tell me that he was yours?"

"What makes you think I knew? And who says that she's telling the truth. That woman can't be trusted. There's no telling how many men she's slept with. Any one of them could be his father."

Peyton stared at him. "Didn't you know?"

"No. Not until Breyonna showed up here. Tell me something, does Liam happen to have a birthmark?"

"A birthmark? Uh, yes. He has a small star-shaped birthmark on his inner right thigh."

Carlton closed his eyes at the same time both his hands covered his face.

"What is it, Carlton?"

"That confirms it more than DNA ever could," he said. "I have the same birthmark in the same place."

She swallowed hard, and her head swooned like she was about to pass out.

Suddenly, they both jumped at the booming sound of an irate female's voice spilling over from the other side of the conference room door.

"Stay here," Carlton ordered Peyton as he jumped up, opened the door, and ran out, slamming the door behind him.

"I told you, lady, I'm not going nowhere. Not until I see Carlton Porter. Do you hear me?"

Carlton heard Breyonna yelling and cussing Jeanine and Mrs. Fentress.

"Call Security," Jeanine ordered Mrs. Fentress.

"Call whoever you want to call. I'm not leaving. Not until I see Carlton."

Carlton bolted toward the sound of the voice.

"What's going on out here?" Carlton asked, almost afraid of the answer he might get from Breyonna.

How dare she just show up at my church. What is she trying to do? Ruin me?

Peyton listened from the conference room. Breyonna had come here? Oh my God, what was she going to do? She cowered behind the door and listened out of sight as best she could.

"You better tell these church groupies of yours to back off," Breyonna warned, spewing an *if-looks-could-kill* kind of scowl on her face. "I swear, you'll be sorry if you don't tell them to back off."

Carlton's palm showed in the air as he halted Mrs. Fentress. "Mrs. Fentress. Jeanine, let me talk to her before you call Security."

Both of the women looked shocked, but they slowly nodded in agreement.

He walked with the quickness up to Breyonna, grabbed her firmly by her elbow, and roughly led her outside the doors of the church while Jeanine and Mrs. Fentress stared on in amazement.

Once outside, he said, "What are you trying to do?" Carlton swore under his breath, still firmly holding on to Breyonna's emaciated arm.

Unsuccessfully, she tried to break free, but Carlton refused to loosen his grip.

"How dare you come here causing a scene. I'm done dealing with your mess. If you don't leave me alone; if you don't get out of my life, I swear as God is my witness..."

"Hah, You? Swearing? A church boy like you?" Breyonna snarled, showing her teeth like a rabid dog. "You go ahead and call Security. Call the police. Call whoever you want to call but I promise you this Carlton Porter, if you and Peyton don't let me see my son in the next twenty-four hours, I'm not only going to the nearest television station, I'm going to be knocking on both you and Peyton's doorsteps, and I'm going to be singing like a bird."

This time Breyonna managed to break free from Carlton. She laughed wickedly as she stormed down the sidewalk leading away from the church.

Carlton watched her as she got inside the same red and black Malibu he'd seen her in before. The driver from what Carlton could tell looked like the same gruffy and unkempt dude.

The car sped off with Breyonna's middle finger raised high up in the air and pointing toward Carlton as the car left the smell of burning rubber behind.

Carlton watched until the car was no longer in his range of vision, then he turned and rushed back inside.

"Are you all right, Pastor?" Jeanine asked.

Visibly shaken, Mrs. Fentress said, "I'll call the police."

"No," Pastor Porter halted her in a biting tone of voice, one that both women were not used to hearing.

Realizing his tone, he spoke in a more calm voice. "Look, no need to call the police. She's gone."

Both of the women's mouths dropped open.

Carlton rushed past Jeanine and Mrs. Fentress and bolted toward the conference room where he'd left Peyton. He didn't stop until he had walked in and closed the door behind him. Then he took in a deep breath before closing his eyes and releasing it.

Peyton rushed up to him.

"We have to tell Derek and Meesha."

"What? Are you serious?"

"And it's time to tell Liam too."

Peyton closed her eyes. The rapid pounding of her heart rendered her helpless. She felt herself slithering to the floor. Suddenly something or someone caught her fall, but not before her eyes closed and her conscious mind drifted to an unknown place. A place that momentarily gave her a means of escape from a life that was rapidly headed on a collision course.

Chapter 29

"But you were always on my mind; you were always on my mind." Brenda Lee

Peyton opened her eyes and woke up to the two busy body women plus another strange woman, all staring at her. She tried to sit up on the sofa that she didn't recall seeing in the conference room until now.

"Feeling better?" the strange woman asked her.

Peyton slowly nodded her head.

"Let me help you sit up. By the way, I'm Lissa. I'm a nurse. I happened to be coming to see my husband, Minister Dalkins. When they told me that someone had fainted, I rushed right over here."

"Thank you," Peyton replied.

"Are you all right?" Carlton asked as he knelt down next to the sofa.

"I'm fine. Just embarrassed. What happened?"

"You passed out."

Peyton continued to look around the room dazed and slightly confused about what had happened. It took her a minute or two to recall the events that had transpired.

"No need to be embarrassed. We just want to know if you're okay. Do you need to see a doctor?" Lissa asked.

"No, I'm good."

Peyton stood up. Still a little shaky and off balanced, she swooned again and Carlton took hold of her waist to help steady her.

"Maybe you should sit back down for a minute. Then I'll drive you home," he told her.

"No, that won't be necessary. I can drive."

"Oh, no. I don't think that's a good idea," added Alissa, the nurse.

"She's right," agreed Mrs. Fentress.

"So, there you have it. You've been outnumbered. I'm going to go get keys. I'll be right back," Carlton told her.

"We'll stay with her until you come back," Jeanine offered.

"Thanks. It won't take but a minute."

■

On the drive home, Peyton and Carlton talked about their common dilemma. Carlton was still reeling from the fact that Breyonna had the audacity to show up at Perfecting Your Faith. This was something serious. Not that he ever thought it was child's play, but now he understood how dangerous Breyonna really could be and he didn't like it, not one bit.

Carlton called one of his trusted staff members who was a detective for the Adverse City Police Department. He told them that Breyonna was a confused, disgruntled woman that came to the church spewing crazy innuendos. The detective told him he would find everything he could about Breyonna and let him know by day's end.

Carlton and Peyton talked at length and decided that they would forego telling Meesha and Derek about Breyonna until after the detective let them know what he came up with, if anything.

"You get some rest and try not to worry," Carlton urged as he pulled into Peyton's driveway. At the same time, one of the church building engineers pulled in the drive behind them driving Peyton's car.

"Thanks, Carlton."

He got out of his car and ran to the passenger side and opened the door for Peyton. He extended his hand toward her. When her car pulled up beside Carlton's, she signaled the driver to park in the circular driveway. He complied.

"Come on, I'll help you inside," Carlton offered.

"No need. I'm straight. Go handle your business. Just call me as soon as you hear from that detective. In the meantime, I'm going to think about what to do next."

Chapter 30

"Do not kid yourself, a conflict is never about the surface issue. It's about ones unsaid, untreated and unhealed wounds." Unknown

A couple of days following the fiasco at Perfecting Your Faith, the housewives met for lunch at one of their usual restaurants. Outside of Peyton, none of the others, including Meesha, were aware of what had occurred.

Meesha was the first to arrive followed by Avery and Eva who came in together.

After they exchanged small talk while looking over the menu, Meesha spoke up. "Have you heard from Peyton? It's not like her not to be here."

"I talked to her briefly a couple of days ago," Avery said.

"Nope, I haven't heard from her. Maybe she's been hitting the sauce a little too much and couldn't drag herself out of the house." Eva joked.

Meesha gave a somewhat disapproving look.

"Well, it's the truth," Eva said. "You know how much she loves to get her drink on."

"Let me call her again," Avery offered, removing her phone from her purse and dialing Peyton's number. "Ummm, it went to voicemail." Avery tried a second time and the same thing happened.

"Call her at home," Meesha said.

Avery made the call to Peyton. "No answer there either. Now I'm starting to worry."

"It's probably nothing. She probably had something else to do today."

"Maybe so," replied Eva.

"Yeah, and she just forgot to tell us," said Meesha.

The housewives ordered their respective foods and after the server left, they continued chatting and catching up on the latest happenings in their lives.

"How are you and Harper getting along?" Meesha asked.

Eva glanced quickly at Avery before responding to Meesha. "We're good. And guess what?" Eva suddenly looked and sounded like she was on cloud nine. "This weekend we're going to the Physician's Ball."

"Ohhhh, that's great. What are you wearing?" Meesha asked.

"Let me guess," chimed in Avery. "Something by Jason Wu."

"How'd you guess?" Eva laughed lightly.

"Because anything that FLOTUS wears, you love. That means if she wears Jason Wu you wear Jason Wu."

Meesha joined in the laughter. "Is she right?"

"You know it," Eva answered.

Meesha's phone rang. She picked it up from the table and answered it. She mouthed to Eva and Avery, "It's Carlton."

After a minute or two of talking to him, she ended the call.

"What was that about?" Avery asked.

"Ummm, I don't really know." She sighed. "He says he needs to talk to me. He wants me to meet him at home in an hour."

"What do you think he wants?" Avery asked.

"Maybe he wants to tell you that he's sorry for acting like such a butthole lately with all that talk about a divorce," Eva said.

"Whatever it is, he sounded serious." Meesha placed her phone inside her purse and then prepared to stand up.

"You aren't going to eat first?" Avery asked, sounding like she was frustrated.

"No, he sounded strange so I want to find out what's going on."

Eva placed her hand on top of Meesha's. "Don't worry. Everything is going to be fine."

Meesha eyed Eva curiously before she smiled. "Thanks. You're right. Anyway, I better go." She opened her purse and removed her American Express Platinum card to pay for her meal.

"Don't bother. I'll take care of it," Avery offered.

"Are you sure?" Meesha asked.

"Yes, now go handle your business. Call and let us know what happened."

"Okay. I'll talk to you ladies later. Oh, and if you hear anything from Peyton, let me know. I hope she's okay."

"Don't worry about Peyton. I'm sure she's fine," Avery told her. "Now go."

Meesha put on her strawberry red caped jacket, picked up her purse and phone, and said her goodbyes to her friends. Whatever Carlton wanted to talk about, she wanted it to be done and over with. From this point forward, she was determined to shake off the worries and give her problems over to God.

■

Carlton made an invisible path across the exquisite dark hardwood floors. Both hands holding his head, eyes closed, fists clinched, lips pursed, and stride hard and heavy. When he heard the ding of the security alarm code being deactivated, he knew it was Meesha. He prepared for the worst. He unclenched his fist, said a silent prayer, exited the room, and went to meet her at the front door. This day was inevitable. It had to happen. Secrets couldn't stay hidden forever.

Leading the way into the kitchen, he walked toward the wraparound kitchen island, stopped, not once deflecting his stare. "I have another kid, a son." There, he'd said it. He'd said it out loud as soon as their eyes bonded.

Meesha felt a flash of hormonal electricity coarse through her body. Carlton had that effect on her. He was highly sexual and his enigmatic aura was magnetic from his confident Obama stride to his Terrence Howard smile. He was an easy man to love. It was the reason she'd bore him four children, and up until recently, she would have gladly given him more.

Did she hear what she thought she heard? *Did Carlton just tell her that he had a son?* She didn't understand what was going on. Of course he had a son. Four of them to be exact.

Meesha remained quiet but confused, watching him from the other end of the kitchen island.

Carlton sounded extremely nervous as she listened to him tell her the story.

"He's about to turn fifteen. Anyway, it was not serious between me and his mother." His stare didn't flinch as he spoke. "This woman, the kid's mother, popped up in Adverse City a few weeks ago, threatening to tell the media and you about him."

Meesha felt her eyes stretch wide open. She imagined she looked like a frog with eyes bulging out of her head. She felt like she was slowly going down a spiral shaped tunnel with a bright light that dimmed as she floated down the tunnel. Her hearing intensified to that of a blind man. She didn't know what to say. She felt like the cat had gotten her tongue.

"How do you know this woman is telling the truth, Carlton? I mean, you're all over the news, TV, the internet, YouTube, the whole gamut because of

Perfecting Your Faith. Flailing her arms, she continued. "How do you know she isn't trying to extort money from you by putting her son off on you? I mean, have you taken a DNA test? I know you aren't going to entertain what she's saying until you know for sure."

For the first time since she entered the room, she captured him with her long legs and svelte body, causing him to lose momentary focus on the conversation at hand. Watching her, she looked somewhat frightened, different from the confident, sexy, and bold woman of faith he knew her to be. Yet, he was still captivated by her beauty.

"I can take a DNA test. I *will* take a DNA test, I should say. I don't think it will prove anything different than what I feel and what I believe."

"And what is it that you believe, Carlton?"

"That Lee…."

"That Liam is his son, Meesha."

Meesha popped around. Her frog like eyes grew even larger when she heard the female's voice and saw the woman who suddenly appeared behind her was Peyton.

"What are you doing?" Carlton exploded. "How did you get in my house?" He looked past Meesha.

Meesha glared. Her eyes tightened. She transferred her hardening stare toward Peyton. An obviously intoxicated Peyton. But intoxicated or not, Meesha entertained every word Peyton said.

"Your hired help let me in, who else. Carlton, I told them. I told Derek and Liam the truth." Peyton sobbed uncontrollably. Her words were thick and slurred. "Derek left me. Liam hates me. They packed their bags and they left me, Carlton. I have nothing left. My son, my husband, they're gone."

"What are you talking about, crazy woman?"

"I'm sorry you had to find out like this, Meesha, but there was no other way."

It's true, Meesha. Well, partially true. Liam may be my kid," Carlton said somberly.

"Liam is your son? How is that? I mean, this can't be real," she said, placing her right hand on her forehead, and her left hand over her belly. "How could you keep something like this from me?" she barked at Carlton. Tears started rising. Her throat felt tight and her head throbbed, not because of pain, but because of anger.

"And you, you slept with my husband?"

"Listen, Meesha." Carlton took several steps toward her.

"Don't come near me. Don't you dare come near me."

"It's not what you think," Peyton said, pleading.

"Shut up. You've already said too much, and on top of that, you're drunk," Carlton accused.

"I may be drunk but I know what I'm saying."

This time it was Meesha who walked toward Carlton. She looked up at him. Who was this man standing in front of her? She thought she knew him. Thought she knew all there was about him like he knew all about her. "You shut up and let her talk," she shouted back, pushing him with the palm of her hand. "I want to hear what this drunken heifer has to say."

"What this drunken heifer has to say is that Carlton is Liam's father." Peyton slurred.

Meesha tried unsuccessfully to keep the tears at bay. She swallowed deeply, hoping it would make the knot forming in her throat disappear.

"He is not *our* son," Carlton barked back.

It was like watching a heated tennis match as her tear-filled eyes flickered back and forth between the two people standing in front of her. Meesha didn't know who to listen to.

Shelia E. Bell

"She is not Liam's mother. At least she's not his birth mother."

"Are you kidding me? Now you want to play me like I'm stupid?" remarked Meesha.

Carlton reached out toward Meesha but she slapped him and quickly stepped away from him.

He rubbed his cheek. "Look, let me explain."

"Explain? I don't think there's anything left to say. You want a divorce so you can be with her?" She looked at Peyton. "And to think, all these years I thought you were my friend. I stood by you, took up for you when everyone else turned their backs on you. And you do something like this?"

Peyton nervously pivoted from one leg to the next.

"Haven't you heard a word I've said? I said that *she*," he pointed at Peyton with a vile angry look on his face, "is not Liam's birth mother. She raised him as her son, that part is true. But Breyonna, his birth mother, gave him to Peyton when Liam was a baby.

"I may not be his biological mother, but he is my child, my son. I know all of this sounds crazy and you may not understand any of it right now, but you deserve to know the truth. And Carlton, I'm sorry, I couldn't keep quiet any longer. I went to the detective and he didn't find anything on her, except some arrests for petty crimes she committed. Don't you see that she's trying to ruin us, and she still can if she goes to the media."

"Get out!" Meesha screamed, stomped, and yelled at Peyton. "Get out of my house now!"

Peyton staggered as she turned to leave. Heavy tears streamed. She ran out the door, leaving it open. She suddenly had a splitting headache. Forget all the commotion going on inside the Porter household. The only thing on her mind was getting in her car and driving home. She needed a drink, an aspirin, and her bed.

166

"Wake up. Peyton, wake up," Derek said. "It's just a dream."

Peyton opened her eyes slowly.

"Are you okay? You were talking and crying in your sleep. Something about Meesha and Liam."

The lingering effects of alcohol remained in her system. Slowly she looked around, and then exhaled deeply. *Thank God,* she thought to herself when she realized she had been dreaming.

Chapter 31

"The saddest thing about betrayal is that it never comes from your enemy." Unknown.

Eva stepped out of the shower, dried herself off, then looked on her vanity for her favorite fragrance. After spraying a dab on each wrist and the center of her neck, she placed the expensive bottle back inside its box. Smiling in the mirror at her slender, perfectly flawless, and statuesque body, she turned around and walked out of the bathroom.

Knock, knock.

The voice stunned her as she came face to face with Seth standing in the hallway at the entrance to her and Harper's master suite.

"Oh, I'm sorry," he said and immediately turned and walked off.

Her skin immediately turned red at the embarrassing thought that Seth had seen her naked. She wasn't used to having to hide behind closed doors. Having him living on their property was a huge change. She quickly rushed over to the door after rushing into her walk-in closet and retrieving a robe. She looked up and down the long hallway to see if he was still around. Not seeing him, she breathed a sigh of relief, then closed and locked her bedroom door.

"What was he doing in the main house anyway? He had everything he could possibly need or want in the guest house."

The ringing phone invaded her thoughts. She walked over to the side of the bed and picked up the phone from its charging cradle. When she saw Harper's name pop up, she smiled, exhaled, and forgot all about Seth.

"Hi," she said in a soft seductive voice.

"Hi, sweetheart. Wow, you sound sexy as hell."

"Oh, do I? How are things going?"

"Good. That's why I was calling. I'm going to get out of here in about an hour. You want to go out for dinner?"

Eva blushed with excitement over the phone. This was the Harper she loved. He could be spontaneous, adventurous, and daring. She loved that about him. "Yes. Of course."

"Okay, I'll see you in a bit."

"I love you, Harper."

"I love you too, baby. I'll be there shortly."

Eva replaced the phone back on its base. She went back to her closet and exchanged her robe for a pair of leggings and an oversized sweatshirt. It was still rather cool outside. Stepping into a pair of sneakers, she left her room and traipsed down the stairs. Looking around when she got to the bottom landing, she saw that the house was empty as she peeped inside several of the rooms, before she went to the side back door leading outside and to the guest house.

"You may be Harper's son but let's get something straight. Do not ever come into my house unannounced again. You are a guest here, not a resident, so don't get it twisted," she said angrily to Seth.

Seth looked stunned.

"Not only should you stay out of our house, especially when Harper isn't home, but you are never to set foot on the second floor of our home ever again. Do I make myself clear?" Eva's voice was so stern and mean that it frightened even her.

"Look, I'm sorry. I was looking for my dad, but you're right. I had no right to be in there. Will you forgive me?"

He sounded rather sad and Eva could see the apologetic look on his face. Now she felt bad that she had gone off on the guy.

"Look, just don't let it happen again," she said, still trying to sound like she was mad.

"I said I was sorry." Seth stared at his father's bombshell wife. He knew it was wrong but he couldn't keep his lustful thoughts at bay. Of course, he really hadn't meant to barge in on her. He really was looking for his dad and he still had to get used to the fact that things around the house were far different than when he visited before. His father had a new wife now and Seth had to remind himself that there was no more free reign for him. But still, he relished in how beautiful Eva was. She had to have married his father for his coins because a woman like her, well, Seth thought there was no way his father was giving her what she needed in the bedroom.

Eva turned to leave.

"You are sexy as hell. But I'm sure my father tells you that all the time." Seth sounded both sarcastic and sincere at the same time.

"Go to hell, Seth."

He couldn't help it. Before he knew it, he came at Eva so fast she had no time to move. He pushed her against the wall and his lips devoured hers as he intertwined his hands in hers and penned both of her hands against the wall.

Eva didn't know what was happening. Why was her body betraying her? Why was she kissing him back? Certainly this couldn't be her voice moaning as Seth's tongue made love to her warm mouth.

"Stop it, you arrogant prick!" She shoved him back with all of her might then looked at him with disgust before she slapped him and ran out of the guest house as fast as she could.

Seth rubbed his stinging face and smiled. "Just as I thought. Dad isn't handling his business."

Back inside the house, Eva's breathing was heavy and her heart was still beating rapidly. She ran upstairs to her bedroom, closed the door, and leaned against it. Rubbing her lips, she could still feel his passion and the heat between them. What had just happened and why had she allowed it? "God, forgive me," she said aloud. "I don't know what that was about." She shook her head like that would make the past moment disappear. She walked over to the bed and stood there replaying what had just happened. She picked up the laced lime-colored Victoria's Secret sheer garter slip off the bed, leaving behind its matching v-string panty. She held the soft material against her skin. "We are going to make a baby tonight, Harper." Eva smiled devilishly as she carried the lingerie back to her closet. She would use it later tonight, but for now, she pushed Seth's kiss out of her mind and proceeded to get dressed. Harper would be home any minute.

■

Spending the evening with Harper was far better than she could ever dream. She forgot all about the kiss she and Seth shared and instead concentrated on the man holding her in his arms as they danced to Tamar Braxton's song *Prettiest Girl*. It reminded her of when she and Harper first met. The long talks, the intimate dinners, him wining and dining her. This was what she had missed, being out with Harper. She convinced herself that the feelings emanating from her when Seth kissed

171

her was only because she missed her husband, missed the feel of his lips pressed against hers and the hardness of his body pressed against her intimate spaces.

"You like this?" Harper seductively whispered while kissing her on the side of her neck as they slow danced. He had to admit that he missed spending time with Eva, but by the same token, he had an obligation to his profession. As much as he loved his wife, his true passion, his lifelong dream was that of being a physician. He couldn't see himself doing anything different. The fact that he was Chief Medical Director at Adverse General was a huge and unexpected blessing in his life. No way could he allow anything to get in the way of his career – not even his young, sexy, beautiful wife. But this evening, unbeknownst to Eva, he had reserved on his calendar to spend time with her. He had to pacify her every now and then if he wanted to keep his marriage intact. That didn't mean that he was ready to give in to her desire to have a baby because he wasn't. Harper wasn't ready to start all over being a father. He made that clear when they first met and started dating. Somewhere along the way, she must have forgotten or pushed it aside, but he hadn't changed his mind. A child meant nothing but responsibility, time and dedication, none of which he was ready to give. His baby was his career.

"I love you so much." Eva looked up at her husband, smiled, and then laid her head against his chest.

Harper kissed the top of her head. "I love you too, sweetheart."

The song ended and they returned to their table. Harper ordered more wine for the two of them. After they danced to a few more songs, they left.

Eva sat close to him in the car as they drove home. She prayed to herself that the rest of the night would be just as magical and perfect as it had already been.

Chapter 32

"Sometimes people are capable of things we never imagined." Unknown.

"I don't know what's up with your girls," Avery said to Eva as both women dined on a salad of mushrooms with fresh herbs and ginger at Zuma's, a high-end Japanese restaurant in Miami. "I've been calling Meesha for the past three days. No answer. When I texted her, it still took forever before she texted back."

"I haven't talked to her either. What did she say when she texted you?"

"She said she and one of the boys were fighting off a cold, and she hadn't felt like talking. Anyway, she said she wouldn't be here today. Said she would fill me in later on some other stuff that was going on."

Eva added, "She's probably still trying to deal with the fact that Carlton wants out of his marriage. I don't know what's up with that man, but I'm telling you, he's a fool. I bet he's messing off with one of those skanks at church who flaunt themselves around the man every chance they get. I've seen how they do. Meesha doesn't want to face the truth."

"I wonder what's going on with Peyton. When I called her, she sounded like she had been on a drinking binge. I could hardly decipher a word she was saying.'

Eva hunched her shoulders and took a bite of her food. "I don't know, but that's her life."

"That's true," Avery cosigned. "Let's change the subject. Is Harper's son still here?"

"Yeah, but he's supposed to be leaving the first of next week. To be honest, I can't wait for him to go, Avery."

"Why? You must think you're not going to be able to control yourself around him much longer." Avery teased. "I have to admit, that boy *is* a real cutie pie." Avery laughed, picked up her glass of white wine, and took a sip.

Almost immediately, Eva's complexion turned from tan to bright red. It was obvious that she was embarrassed.

"What's wrong? Did I hit a nerve?"

"No, it's not that, but I do have something I want to tell you. You're the only one I can trust to not say a word."

Avery leaned in closer, curious about what Eva had to say. "What is it?" She placed a forkful of her food inside of her mouth.

"Seth kissed me."

As quickly as Avery inserted her food, just as quickly, she almost expelled it. She put her hand up to her mouth, as her tight eyes suddenly grew large. "He what?"

"You heard me correctly. He kissed me."

"Tell me the details, girl," Avery urged.

"It happened the other day. I was about to get ready for my date with Harper."

Avery's palm halted Eva's words. "Hold up. A date with Harper? I can't believe I miss a couple of days talking to you and all of this happens. I knew Harper would make things right with you. The man loves you, Eva. But anyway, forget that for now. Keep talking."

Eva told Avery everything about how it all went down. "I feel so guilty, Avery. I love Harper so why didn't I stop Seth? What's wrong with me?"

Avery was sympathetic to her friend. "Let's examine the situation. First of all, you're human. Seth is a good-looking man. You two are almost the same age. Harper is never around. You've been lonely for a long time. And let's not talk about the fact that you've told me numerous of times that you and Harper rarely make love. It's no wonder that you enjoyed the touch of a man."

"But he's Harper's son. I feel horrible."

"You shouldn't. I'm not condoning what he did because he was out of line. But then again, you're a beautiful woman, Eva. The man isn't blind, for goodness sakes. You know the deal. You're not green."

Eva looked down and away from Avery. Sighing, she bit lightly on her lip before looking up again. "It's just that I can't believe that I actually enjoyed his kiss, that I didn't push him off."

"Get over it. Anyway, you just said he'll be leaving in a few days. Let it go. Now tell me about you and Harper."

"Honeee, if that man didn't make up for all the nights he's left me to share our bed all by my lonesome. I'm telling you, he made me feel some type of way. We went to dinner, dancing, and then when we got home we danced between the sheets all night. It was everything I could imagine, girl." Eva had a broad smile spread across her face as she talked. "I hope we made a baby. I pray that we did."

Avery pushed her plate back, picked up her table napkin, and gently wiped her mouth.

Eva basically followed suit and did the same when the server approached their table. "Check please," Eva told the young male server.

After he turned around and left, Avery spoke up. "What do you think Harper is going to say, or should I say, *do*, if you *are* pregnant?"

"I don't know, but like you told me, he'll get over it. We love each other. And he knows how badly I want a child."

"I agree. He'll give you the cold shoulder for a minute and then when that precious little child enters into this world, all will be forgiven." Avery shrugged her shoulders. "But, hey, if he chooses his career over his family, then that will be his loss, not yours."

Eva looked at Avery with admiration. "You are such a good friend. Thank you, Avery, but believe me, I can handle Harper Stenberg."

The ladies paid their checks, got up, and left the restaurant to go shopping. While shopping, Avery's phone rang.

"Hi, I was wondering if you wanted to meet me downtown for lunch in about an hour."

Avery looked over at Eva. She put her phone on Mute. "It's Ryker. He wants to meet for lunch."

"Tell him that you'll meet him."

"But...."

"But nothing. Tell him, yes."

She unmuted the phone and replied, "Uh, sure."

"Did you have other plans? You sound apprehensive," he said.

"Uh, no. But I guess you can say that I am surprised, but it's a pleasant surprise. Anyway, I'll see you soon.

"Cool, meet me at Jaya."

"Jaya? The new restaurant inside The Setai Hotel?"

"You got it."

"My, my my. That sounds great."

"Good. See you in a little bit."

"Okay. Buh-bye." Avery pushed the End button and turned to look at Eva who was grinning. "You're laughing? I can't believe you. I'm stuffed. How am I going to eat again?"

"Easy, just get something light. You can work the extra calories off in no time. The important thing is for you to get out of here and go meet your husband. It sounds like he's trying to bring the spark back into your marriage."

"I think it might be too late for that. There was a time, and not long ago either, when I prayed that things would work out. But to be honest, now I don't know if I even want this relationship anymore."

"I think you still love him. It's just that you've been hurt. But you should at least give him credit for trying to make things right, and why wouldn't he? He's the one who committed adultery."

"Yeah, I guess," Avery said, sounding disinterested and detached.

Eva and Avery walked in silence to the parking garage and found their respective cars.

"Have fun," Eva told Avery as she walked off, leaving Avery with butterflies forming in her belly at the thought that she was having lunch with the man of her dreams.

Avery had been praying for a change in her life. Every Sunday that she sat in church listening to Carlton talk about God's unconditional love, little by little she began to forgive herself for the mistakes of her past. She had carried guilt around long enough. If she was ever going to make her life better and be the kind of mother her girls deserved, she had to get herself together. She prayed and asked God to change her mindset. Slowly things seemed to get somewhat better. She and Ryker weren't exactly lovey-dovey toward each other, but they were getting along far better than they had in a long time. Avery felt that it was because she no longer cared whether things worked out between them or not. She no longer cared about him making her his wife either, now that she'd found love in the arms of another.

Avery had Carlton to thank for her change of heart. He may have had his own issues, but when he stood in the pulpit of Perfecting Your Faith and delivered the Word of God, lives were changed and souls were saved. He had a way of speaking faith into people, of renewing their hope with his powerful messages. It took some time, but Avery decided that she was no longer going to allow her past to dictate her future. For the first time in her life, she began to believe that God really did love her, something she hadn't always believed.

As for Ryker, he loved his girls but did he love Avery? He'd asked himself that question over and over again. Especially since he'd never wifed her, and he didn't know if he ever would. What he did know was that he didn't want his girls growing up without both parents. He'd seen more than his share of failed relationships. He believed that once two people married, it should be for a lifetime, through thick and thin, better or worse. He was unsure if he wanted to go there with Avery. His mother and father would be married forty-seven years in a couple of months. They were still just as much in love now as they were when they first met. The same wasn't true for him and Avery. How much of the love he once felt for her could be salvaged, Ryker didn't know, but what he did know was that he was going to try to make things better between him and Avery. They certainly had their share of life's ups and downs. Through it all they had been blessed with Lexie and Heather. They had no financial concerns and Ryker remained determined to provide the best of everything for his daughters. Maybe, just maybe, he could make her his wife, but he still needed a little more time.

■

Arriving at the hotel restaurant, Avery cautiously looked around as she walked inside. "Hi," Avery said, walking up to the table located in a private dining section of the restaurant.

Carlton pushed back from the table, stood up, and kissed her on the cheek. "Hi," he said.

Avery blushed.

Carlton pulled out a chair for her and waited until she sat down before he helped bring her in closer to the table.

Avery understood that in a sense she was doing to Meesha what Olivia had done to her, but sleeping with Carlton wasn't something she'd set out to do, it just happened. Yet, at this point, Avery didn't care. After being unhappy with Ryker for quite a while, Carlton made her happy, and it was a good feeling. When Carlton told her that he was in love with her and was going to divorce Meesha, initially Avery tried to talk him out of it, but he refused to change his mind. Avery didn't want to see Meesha hurt, and she felt bad for her, but there was no way she was going to give up the love that she and Carlton had found in one another.

As for Ryker, Avery once loved him with all of her heart and soul, but now that love was gone. And if he loved her so much, he would have married her by now and he definitely wouldn't have cheated. But all of that was in the past because her heart belonged to none other than Carlton Porter.

When Avery and Ryker first met, he was attentive, romantic, and considerate. He wined and dined her and presented her with lavish gifts. When they consummated their relationship, she found him to be a skilled lover, which made her fall more deeply in love with him. In less than two years, they were engaged and he had put a rock on her finger that sparkled like the sunlight. Yet, he never married her and every time she talked about it, he found some excuse as to why the time wasn't right. She blamed herself for being absorbed with her own life and being way too insecure. She was a nagger too because she hated that his law practice took up so much of his time. The more she hounded him, the further he withdrew. But it seemed like the mistakes they both made in their relationship were behind them now and Ryker was ready to make things better, but Avery wasn't.

"You look lovely," Carlton told her, smiling at Avery and reaching across the table to caress her fingertips.

She blushed again. "Thank you." She took the white cloth napkin, unfolded it, and placed it on her lap.

The server appeared and Carlton ordered coffee for himself and for Avery, he ordered one of her favorites, a blend of strawberry, peach, and citrus tea.

"How was your morning?" she asked him as the server returned with a cup of hot brewed tea and Carlton's coffee.

The server took their orders, and they resumed their conversation after he left.

"There's a lot going on right now. I've been dealing with some major issues," he explained.

"Major issues? Like what?" Avery asked. "For how long?"

"Things have been crazy for a few weeks at least," Carlton said. "The drama never ends."

"Are you okay? Do you want to talk about it? Is it something going on at church?"

"I guess you can say that the church could be brought into it. I expect some things are probably going to come out in the media soon." Carlton rubbed his head and shook his head.

"What is it, baby?" Avery asked. "You know you can talk to me about anything."

"Yeah, I know. That's one of the reasons I'm so crazy about you. You're a good listener. A man of God needs someone that he can confide in and lean on sometimes. You know what I mean?"

"Yes, I do." Avery nodded.

"I've found that in you. I can't thank you enough for being the wonderful person that you are, Avery, which is why I have to come clean with you about what's going on in my life."

Carlton told Avery everything that was going on. When he finished, Avery sat in silence. She couldn't believe it. Liam was his son? Hearing this rattled her somewhat, but it didn't change what she felt for Carlton. As crazy as it sounded, Avery believed that everything would somehow work out. She encouraged Carlton not to cave under the pressure, to keep his focus and faith on God, and to remember that he had her by his side.

"See that's why I fell in love with you. You make being with you so easy. You don't judge me. You accept me for who I am. I'm a man of God, but I'm an average man first," he told her. "And this average man has something he wants to give to you."

"Give me? What is it?" Avery asked, looking surprised.

Carlton smiled warmly, reached inside the left pocket of his jacket, and pulled out a small blue velvet box. He placed it gently on the table and eased it in front of Avery.

Looking stunned, Avery's eyes widened, and her mouth upturned. "What is this?

"It's for you. Open it," Carlton told her.

With trembling hands, she proceeded to open it. Her mouth opened wider than her eyes as she surveyed the diamond Tiffany line bracelet.

"Oh, my God, it's beautiful, Carlton."

She removed the bracelet from the box and studied it with pleasure as it sparkled brightly.

Carlton removed the bracelet from her hands and placed it on her dainty wrist.

"So you like it, huh?"

"Do I *like* it? I love it. But…I mean, why? What's it for?"

"What's it for? I'll tell you what it's for." First Carlton leaned in and kissed her, not caring who might recognize them. "It's for the woman I love. Every time you put this on I want it to remind you of how much you mean to me."

"Oh, Carlton, I love you, babe. I love you so much."

"Why don't we hurry up and eat so we can get out of here. I can think of something better the two of us can spend our time doing. What do you say?" Carlton winked.

"I have a better idea. Let's get the server to prepare our food to go." Avery smiled seductively.

After they got their food packed in to-go boxes, Avery followed Carlton to the elevator leading to the room he had reserved at the five-star luxury hotel. For the next few hours, the couple made love. As she lay in his arms, she tried to reassure him again that she would do whatever she could to help him through the ordeal with Breyonna, with Meesha, and with Peyton. She may have had her own set of problems, but the problems she was going through with Ryker were nothing compared to what was unraveling in her lover's life. She would definitely have to stay on her knees on behalf of Carlton Porter.

■

At home, after she returned from being with Carlton most of the afternoon, she prepared dinner, helped the girls with their homework, and finally got the chance to relax. Ryker was still at the office so she had time to bathe in the memories she had made with Carlton. She placed her hands on her tummy as she laid on her back across the bed. When they were together earlier, she started to tell Carlton the news but decided that she would wait a little longer before telling him. She wanted everything to be perfect, just right, before she let him know that she was carrying his love child. She toyed with the bracelet he had brought her as her smile broadened.

Later that evening, when Ryker came home, for some weird reason, he wanted to talk. Avery didn't care to hear anything he had to say, but he insisted.

"We're both to blame for our shaky relationship," Ryker told her as he sat on the bed next to her. "But at the end of the day, I want you to know that I do love you. I really do. And I've been praying every day that you would forgive me."

"I do forgive you, and I've been reevaluating my life, too, Ryker. Thanks to Pastor Porter and his powerful messages, I've come to realize and understand that we have to let go of the past and live for today. Tomorrow is not promised and neither of us should want to live a life that's predicated on past failures and mess-ups."

"That's exactly what I wanted to hear. I think we can make this work, Avery. I want us to get married."

Avery sat in silence. Ryker wanted to give their relationship another chance. Avery smiled within herself.

"What do you have to say?" he asked her.

Avery looked at him head on and without so much as a flinch, she said, "I want out."

Chapter 33

"Deception may give us what we want for the present, but it will always take it away in the end." Richard Hawthorne

Eva was both nervous and excited at the same time. Her period was over a week late. She hadn't told Harper that she had stopped taking the pill. He would be upset if he knew, but if she was pregnant, Harper would be just fine. She believed that with all of her heart. After a little less than three minutes, the word PREGNANT appeared in the test strip window.

Eva squealed and jumped up and down in the bathroom. She couldn't wait to share the news, so she decided to call Avery. As for Harper, she wanted to make her announcement special. She would have their personal chef to prepare his favorite dish and serve it over candlelight.

She called Avery but she didn't answer so she left a voicemail. "Avery, call me. I have something to tell you." After she ended the call, she then followed up with a text. Next, she contacted her mom via Skype to tell her the news. Harper had purchased her parents a computer so they could keep in touch with their daughter. Her mother was illiterate but Eva had a younger brother who showed her parents how to communicate using the computer.

When Eva told her mother that she was pregnant, she was happy for Eva, but she questioned about whether or not Harper would feel the same. Eva tried to reassure her that he would be just fine, especially after the baby arrived. Everything would be perfect. It had to be.

"I don't know if my father is going to be overly joyous about having another kid."

Shelia E. Bell

Startled, Eva quickly turned and faced Seth. "What are you doing in this house? I told you not to come in here when Harper isn't home."

"Hey, look, I only came to tell you that I'm out of here. I'm headed back home."

"Oh, good for you. Well, have a safe trip." Eva looked and sounded awkward. Seth made her a little nervous. It wasn't that she was frightened of him or anything like that, it was because she would only admit to herself that she felt an attraction towards him whenever he was around.

"Look, I think you've made a mistake getting pregnant. I know my father, and having a kid is not something he wants."

"What were you doing? Eavesdropping? You have some nerve. But let me say this. I think I know better than you what my husband does and doesn't want. I don't need you, or anyone else, to tell me anything. And I would appreciate it if you would keep your mouth shut. I'm Harper's wife, and I'll be the one to let him know that he's going to be a father."

"What did you say?"

Eva stumbled backwards at the sound of Harper's voice booming like rolling claps of thunder as he suddenly appeared inside the open entrance of the family room.

"Harper? What are you doing home?"

"I live here."

"I know that. I mean, you're home early."

"I came to see my son off." Harper looked over at Seth who was standing in front of Eva, slightly to the right.

Eva looked at Seth. He shook his head in slow motion, and positioned his lips in a way that revealed he actually felt bad for his stepmother, but Seth knew his

186

father and understood all too well that what he said, Harper Stenberg meant. And if his father told Eva that he did not want children, then nothing or no one was going to make him feel differently.

"Oh, of course," Eva stated.

"What did I hear you say?"

Eva smiled, looked down, and placed her hand over her belly. Looking back up and at Harper, she said while continuing to smile, "We're going to have a baby." She ran to Harper and fell against his chest.

Harper, almost violently, pushed her off him. With eyes that seemed to have turned from bright white to blood red, he glared at her.

Frightened, Eva took an extra step backwards, but kept her eyes glued on Harper. She had never seen him look or sound like this and it terrified her.

"Pack your stuff." His voice was scary calm.

"Where are we going?" she asked.

"On second thought, don't bother. I'll make sure all of your things are properly packed and delivered."

Eva smiled. "Oh, baby, I knew you would be happy. Where are you taking me?"

Harper said nothing and neither did Seth. The two men kept staring at Eva.

After he didn't respond but kept staring, Eva spoke up again. "Harper, you're scaring me. I don't understand."

"Well, let me see if I can help you understand more clearly." He spoke sternly. "I told you from the beginning my feelings about having more children. I made it clear that I did not want another kid."

"I know, Harper," Eva said pitifully, "but you know how much I wanted a baby. I love you, honey. And I know you'll love our child more than life itself." She massaged her belly in a circular motion.

"I want you out of here. And I want you out now." His voice turned calm again, but cold. "You can use the credit card to get yourself a hotel room. I don't care what you do as long as you leave and don't you ever show your face around here again," he fumed.

"Harper. Please. I don't think you know what you're saying." She began to cry.

"Oh, I know exactly what I'm saying; you're going to get out of my house. I don't care where you go. Go to the father of that baby you're carrying."

"What? I can't believe you. I know you can't be trying to say that this baby isn't yours." Eva held her stomach.

"I'm not *trying* to say anything, I said it!" snapped Harper. "That kid in your belly is not mine."

"Why are you saying these things? You know I wouldn't mess around on you. I love you, Harper." Eva continued to cry.

Seth stood to the side quietly, looking like he felt sorry for her.

"You're a lying slut," Harper accused.

"No I'm not. Please stop this crazy talk."

"That kid is not mine," Harper said again.

"But it is, Harper," Eva insisted.

Harper yelled. "I'm sterile, Eva. I had a vasectomy five years ago."

Eva swooned as lightheadedness came over her. Her eyes locked with Seth's as she steadied herself to keep from falling.

■

Seeing the look on Eva's face had told Harper everything he needed to know. It hurt him to the core to know that the woman he loved had betrayed him, cheated on him, and was now carrying another man's seed. It was

188

over between them. If she wanted him to, he would send her back to Bolivia. He didn't care anymore. There was nothing further for them to build on. She didn't love him, no matter how many times she said that she did. After all, the best proof of love is trust.

Chapter 34

"Bad is never good until worse happens." Unknown

"I am not going to do it," Peyton told Breyonna, while she sat in the front and Breyonna sat fidgeting around in the back seat of Carlton's silver Tesla. "You can go to the media, do whatever you want to do, I don't care. I've made up my mind, and you are not going to disrupt Liam's life. You will not see my son!"

"Calm down, Peyton." Carlton reached over and squeezed her hand gently.

"And you think going to the tabloids won't disrupt his life, you big dummy," retorted Breyonna. "You must not love the boy like you pretend that you do."

"Look, Breyonna, no need for name calling. Here, take this and leave. Leave *me* alone. Leave *Peyton* alone and go back to Memphis or wherever. There's twenty-five thousand dollars in there, enough for you to go and get yourself a decent place to live and get your life back on track."

Breyonna snatched the leather pouch that had the money tucked away inside. "Y'all are more desperate than I thought," she said, laughing wickedly. "But I ain't complaining. You better be glad I changed my mind and decided to take this money."

"Yeah, we're both glad you decided to accept our help," Carlton said, hoping his calm demeanor would pacify her and she would leave him and Peyton alone.

"I'll go." She proceeded to open the back door. "But you know what, one day the truth is going to come out, and Peyton, you're going to be sorry that you didn't tell Liam about me. The same goes for you, Carlton. No secret stays hidden forever. Just you wait and see."

"You just keep your mouth shut," Peyton said angrily. "Let me worry about my future."

Carlton continued his stoical demeanor. "Look at it this way, Breyonna. Probably for the first time, you're thinking about someone other than yourself. In this instance it's your son you're thinking about, and that's a good thing. He's a good kid. We don't need to mess that up. Like they say, let sleeping dogs lie."

"Yeah, whateva. I'm outta here," Breyonna said and jumped out of the car, leaving the door open.

Carlton got out, shut the door and watched Breyonna and her friend speed off the parking lot of the restaurant where they'd met up.

"Do you think she's out of our lives for good?" Peyton asked.

"I don't know, all I can do is pray that she is. She doesn't want Liam, not after all this time. All she ever wanted was what I gave her – money."

Peyton started crying.

"Why are you crying?" Carlton asked.

"I want this whole thing to be over, Carlton. I just want to go on with my life. My son means everything to me, and if he ever finds out that I kept the truth from him, he'll hate me. Oh, God, how could I mess up my life like this?"

"Look," Carlton said, stroking her shoulder. "Everything is going to be fine. She's gone. We have to have faith that she's gone for good. Look how long it took her to show up anyway. I'm telling you, all she ever wanted was the money, not Liam. Now pull yourself together, and go home to your son and your husband. Okay?"

Peyton looked at Carlton, and managed a forced smile as he began to wipe her tears away.

He leaned in and kissed her lightly and quickly on the lips. "Thank you for being such a good mother to my kid. I owe you. I owe you big time," Carlton said.

Peyton went inside her handbag, pulled out some tissue, and wiped her remaining tears away. Carlton was right. Breyonna got what she came for and now she was gone. Finally, she could exhale, go home, and make herself a good strong drink.

■

"How'd it go?" Breyonna's boyfriend asked, as she sat in the car.

Overjoyed, she responded, "We're in the money, baby. Let's get outta here and go back home to Memphis unless you wanna hang around here for a minute."

"I do kinda like it here," he told her. "This is good living. Now that you got a little something, we can do some thangs."

"Yeah, we can do a lot of thangs," Breyonna agreed. "I think you might have a point. I agree we stay here, at least for a while. That way I'll be close by my kid, and some more of this." She giggled and made it rain with money inside the car.

"I like the sound of that. So where to now?" he asked, steering the Malibu out into the street.

"The news station," Breyonna said. "You know what they say, one should always have multiple streams of income."

Chapter 35

"Beware of keeping secrets, because surely what's done in the dark will eventually come to the light." D. Smith

Meesha's cell phone rang, then rang again. Next, her text notifier chimed. "What is going on?" she said aloud to herself. Stopping at the traffic light, she put the phone on Drive Mode and proceeded to M. E. Porter Independent School. The school, named after her, had been a dream of hers for many years, so when Carlton told her that he was going to start the school three years prior, she was enthralled. She spent countless hours helping with the interior layout and design of the school whose grades ranged from kindergarten through grade eight. Meesha also assisted with a school curriculum that focused on providing the students with a world-class education in both Creative and Performing Arts and Enriched Academics. The tuition to attend the private school was steep but the school offered a number of scholarships to children of members of Perfecting Your Faith.

This was the first school year that the new state of the art building was open, housing grades six through eight.

She arrived at the school, there to pick up the boys. She parked her car in the space reserved for her, and strutted inside the newly constructed school building. Meesha smiled as she walked along the corridor, peering briefly inside some of the classrooms as she made her way to her oldest son's classroom first.

She exchanged friendly conversation with his teacher and then proceeded to the area that housed the lower grades.

After she picked up the boys, Meesha drove toward their home in the prestigious neighborhood of Benton

Heights. Her oldest son's cell phone rang just as she drove into her parking spot inside their four-car garage.

"Mom, it's dad on the phone. He wants to talk to you."

Carlton, Jr. passed the phone to her.

"Hello."

"I've been trying to reach you for the last forty five minutes," Carlton said, sounding nervous. "Is everything okay?"

"Everything's fine. I just picked up the boys, now I'm pulling up at home. My phone is still in Drive Mode. What's so urgent that you had to call me on Carlton's phone. Is everything alright?"

The boys opened the car doors and started getting out.

She paused from talking to Carlton. "You all go inside and start on your homework," she told them.

"So you've already left the school?" he asked. "It's early."

"They get out at one o'clock on Wednesdays. Remember?"

"Oh, yeah, that's right."

"What's up?" she asked.

"I wanted you to run by the church. But, never mind, I'll talk to you when I get home. I should be there in a few."

"Are you sure? I can drive back over there. Just give me a minute to tell Yulisa that I'm going back out." Yulisa was the children's nanny and she often prepared meals for the family.

"No, no, no. Don't come all the way back here."

"You sound worried. Tell me what's wrong, Carlton?"

He paused before speaking. "Like I said, we'll talk when I get there. I'll see you soon."

"Okay. I love—," Meesha expressed only to hear the phone click in her ear. "Carlton? Hello?"

Meesha held the phone as she made her way inside the house.

On her way to take Carlton, Jr. his phone, she spoke her version of Luke 112 verse seven, a scripture she'd memorized and often recited whenever she felt herself becoming anxious or worried. "I will not be afraid of bad news; my heart is firm, because I trust in you Lord."

Meesha took Carlton Jr. his phone and took hers off of Drive Mode. She started scrolling through it, looking at all the calls she had received as well as the text messages.

`Answer your phone!` A text message said.

`Urgent,` another one said. `Go online and watch the local news` still another one said. There were several more, all from different people.

Meesha grew nervous. Instead of going to the kitchen to see if Yulisa was in there, she went upstairs to her office, closed the door, and sat down at her desk. She turned on her computer and proceeded to go online. Her hand went over her heart when she saw the article and began reading it.

Adverse City, FL Carlton H. Porter, Senior Pastor & Founder of Perfecting Your Faith Ministry has teen love child with millionaire socialite, Peyton Hudson, Wife of Adverse City National Bank President, Derek Hudson. Sources say....

This was the reason he had called and wanted her to come by the church. He was trying to get to her before she found out the truth from the tabloids!

Meesha suddenly felt ill, like she was about to faint. What was she going to do now? She was pregnant with her and Carlton's fifth child. The timing couldn't be worse. She hadn't told anyone the news yet. She'd just found out herself a few days ago. She must have gotten pregnant that day Carlton and her made love in his study. This nightmare seemed to be just beginning and she didn't know what to believe or who to believe. Meesha didn't know when would be the right time to spill the beans. For now, her being pregnant had to remain her secret and hers alone. Things were already complicated enough and now that she was pregnant, it would complicate matters even more. "God, what am I supposed to do if this stuff I'm reading is all true. No wonder Carlton wants a divorce. He knew this was going to come out. Oh, Lord, noooo," she screamed and cried while holding her hand over her mouth. "Carlton and Peyton? A son? Lord, this doesn't make sense. It just doesn't," she sobbed and pleaded. "Please, God, not this."

Chapter 36

"Some secrets are meant to be known but once known you can never forget them." Pseudonymous Bosch

Almost a week had passed since the media frenzy started. Reporters camped outside the gated community like vultures, waiting on the Porter family to appear from behind the gates. Calls from Perfecting Your Faith informed Carlton that reporters were popping up there as well. The news about Carlton and Peyton had gone viral. The house phone rang incessantly.

Meesha paced across the massive span of dark hardwood floors. She had eaten very little and hadn't had a restful night's sleep in days. She didn't return the endless phone calls and texts from church members, family and the housewives. For now, she needed some time to herself. It was bad enough that she and Carlton were going at it like wild cats and dogs. She had to shield her kids from the madness that was circling around their family too. It was downright hard and so far she hadn't been able to keep them from hearing the stories that circulated. All she could do was her best not to make their father look like a bad person. They loved their dad, and no matter what he'd done, he loved his boys. He was a good father to them, but a lousy, cheating husband to her.

Meesha's text notifier chimed. It was Peyton again, pleading with her to give her a chance to explain what happened. Meesha had had enough. She blocked Peyton's number. It was too late for explaining. The devil was busy, and Meesha didn't think she had the strength, faith, or courage to fight him off right now.

"Mrs. Porter, Mrs. Stenberg is here to see you. I told her you weren't seeing anyone, but she insisted. She says

197

Shelia E. Bell

she isn't leaving until she talks to you," Meesha's housekeeper informed her.

"I don't care what she said; I don't want to see anyone."

"You're going to see *me*," Eva said, bolting pass the housekeeper. "What's going on with you?"

"I'm sorry, Mrs. Porter," the housekeeper said. "Please, you have to leave," she said to Eva.

"It's okay, I'll handle it," Meesha told the middle-aged woman.

The housekeeper nodded then turned to leave.

"I don't appreciate you just popping up over my house."

"If you think I was going to stay away with everything that's happening, you're crazy. I'm your friend, Meesha. I'm not going to let you go through this by yourself." Eva's voice sounded sympathetic.

Suddenly Meesha broke down in tears. She held her head inside her hands and bawled.

Eva rushed toward her and immediately embraced her distraught friend.

"I'm so sorry, Meesha. I've been trying to get in touch with you since I heard about what went down."

"It's horrible. I don't know how I'll ever get through this, Eva."

"I don't want to hear you talk like that," Eva rebutted. "How many times have you said that God will never leave us hanging? You have an invincible type of faith and no matter how tough things are right now, you're going to make it through. Anyway, do you really think it's true, you know…what they're saying?" Eva asked.

"I wish it wasn't, but according to Carlton, it's all true, except for the part about him and Peyton sleeping together. He says that never happened, and that the chick who went to the media with all this stuff lied about that

198

part. But why would I believe him, since he's been lying all these years about Peyton's child, or adopted child, or whoever the boy belongs to. I knew he and Peyton were friends in college, but I didn't know they used to mess around. I'm so confused. I don't know what to believe anymore."

Eva placed her arms around Meesha, hoping to comfort her in some small way. "You heard from Avery?"

"No. I haven't talked to anyone; I don't want to."

"So you're saying you believe Liam really is Carlton's biological son?"

"Yes. He basically admitted it. He says Peyton isn't the reason he wants a divorce, but I don't believe that either. And let's not even go there when it comes to that drunk. She's just as much a liar as he is, telling us that story about adopting that boy and his parents being dead. Imagine what it's doing to Liam? And Derek, too."

"All of this is crazy. I'm shocked. I just can't wrap my mind around it. And here I was feeling sorry for myself."

Meesha looked up at Eva. "Why? What's going on with you?"

"Never mind me. We'll talk about that later. Right now, I want you to lie down and try to get some rest. You look like you haven't slept in ages."

"I haven't." Meesha burst out in tears. She took a seat in a chair and sobbed into her hands. "I hate him, Eva. And Peyton, how could she smile up in my face knowing she's been screwing my husband behind my back."

"This is low even for Peyton. I can't get over that two faced, lying wench. How could she do this to you? And for all these years? No wonder she drinks like she does; she knows she's been sleeping with the enemy while smiling up in your face." Eva's accent grew thicker with each word she spoke. She'd temporarily forgotten about her own situation. "Don't cry, Meesha."

"I don't know what I'm going to do. I knew he wanted out of the marriage, but this is unbelievable. I feel like I'm having a nightmare." She boo-hooed.

"Where is Carlton now?" Eva asked.

"We've been going at it nonstop. It's been bad. Really bad."

"Where is he?" Eva asked her again.

"He left. Who would have thought that he could lie so easily, Eva? And how could I be so stupid and blind?"

Eva sat down next to Meesha, leaned slightly over, rested her elbows on her legs, and clasped her hands. "Dang, life is so unfair," she said, as her own tears flowed.

■

After her visit with Meesha, Eva went back to her hotel suite and did what she did almost every night since she checked in—and that was cry. Harper refused to talk to her ever since he threw her out of their home. He had put her up in one of the best hotels on Fisher Island, gave her some money and unlimited use of one of the credit cards to live off, but other than that, he wouldn't have anything to do with her. He wouldn't answer her calls, changed the access key to their property, and banned her from the hospital. When she told Avery what happened, Avery tried her best to comfort her but with everything that had been going on in Avery's own life, it was hard for her to provide any source of undivided comfort to Eva.

Eva sat on the sofa and blindly studied the room service menu, without any intention of ordering from it. She was lonely, lost, and felt all alone. She couldn't believe that Harper had kept the fact that he had a vasectomy a secret. How could he do something like that? She didn't know where his mind was at. Was he going to divorce her or would he cool off and then allow her to talk things out with him? She loved Harper and she believed he loved her. Surely, he would come to terms with the fact that this was partially his fault, and not just hers alone. He was the one who shut her out and put his career first. He was the one who left her aching for him sometimes weeks at a time. She was young and she needed to be loved and treated with affection, something that Harper rationed out like it was the middle of the Great Recession.

The fact that she had betrayed Harper was something she had to deal with all by herself. No one knew that she'd been unfaithful to her marriage, not Avery and not Meesha. She also hadn't told them that Harper was sterile. They only knew that he had kicked her to the curb when she told him she was pregnant. Her heart was broken and she felt like her life was falling apart. She could understand what drove Avery to try to kill herself, because she was just as depressed. If it wasn't for the baby she was carrying, maybe she would have committed suicide. Then again, even if she wasn't pregnant, she couldn't do something like that. She believed that God would never forgive her if she took her own life.

Eva got up from the sofa and went into the hotel bedroom, laid back on the bed, turned on her side, and balled up in a fetal position. Her life was ruined. Her parents, especially her mother, were going to be so disappointed in her. Her mother had her concerns about Harper from the beginning, and now Eva could understand why. He had no right to keep something like this from her. She wondered what other things he may be hiding, and why he was so quick to throw her out.

201

Something wasn't adding up, but what could she do about it? She had messed up in a huge way, and deep down inside she knew she had no one to blame but herself.

Meesha thought *she* was living a nightmare, but if only she knew what Eva was experiencing. Eva wanted to tell Meesha that she was going through something a thousand times worse. She thought back to what Harper said: "That kid can't be mine. It's impossible because I can't have children. I had a vasectomy…'"

Chapter 37

"In life, we never lose friends; we only learn who the true ones are."

Breyonna sat alone in her jail cell waiting on her trial for attempted murder, which ironically had nothing to do with Carlton, Peyton, or her son. She and the man in the Chevy Malibu got into a huge fight over drugs and the small sum of money she had left from what Carlton gave her. She stabbed him several times, and almost killed him. He lay in the Critical Care Unit at Adverse General Hospital in grave condition. The knife had penetrated some of his vital organs, and it was still uncertain if he would survive.

∎

Carlton sat in his office at Perfecting Your Faith reading the latest news, and checking to see what else the media was saying about him. The swarm of media that had been surrounding his neighborhood and his church had dwindled down to one or two during the course of a day. Maybe he could get his life back to some semblance of order. Now that Breyonna was in jail, he felt like he could at least breathe a little easier. She had no money for the $250,000 bond that had been set for her, so she would be locked up for a long while. That would give him time to concentrate on moving ahead with the divorce from Meesha and make a life with a woman who needed him and adored him. Meesha was too perfect in his eyes. She acted like she could do no wrong. She reminded him of the women on the old movie, "The Stepford Wives." He cared for her a lot, and she was still beautiful and sexy, but he didn't want to remain married to her. He couldn't explain it, he just knew that their relationship as they'd known it all these years, was no more. His heart belonged to Avery, someone who needed him for a change. He felt like he could make things better for her by treating her with the love she deserved.

"Pastor Porter, turn on the news. They're talking about that woman who came here and caused all that commotion a few weeks ago. Hurry up, they're holding a news conference about her now," his administrative assistant rushed in his office and told him.

Jeanine turned on the television in Carlton's office. He turned around in his chair and began listening to the Chief of Police as he talked about the death of Breyonna Walker.

"At about 7:10 a.m., cell check revealed inmate Breyonna Walker was alive and well. At about 8:46, officers reported they found her unresponsive in her jail cell with a stab wound to the heart. CPR was performed on Walker and she was rushed to Adverse General Hospital where she was pronounced dead...No one has been charged at this time."

Jeanine, with arms folded, stood near Carlton's office door watching the news conference along with him. Her eyes were glued to the small flat screen and her ears were tuned in so she wouldn't miss a beat.

Carlton took in each word being said. *Breyonna? Dead?*

"If you'll excuse me, Jeanine."

"Oh, yes sir. I'm sorry. I didn't mean to stay in here. I just got caught up watching this." Jeanine exited Carlton's office, closing the door behind her.

Carlton reached on the side of his desk for his phone and quickly called Peyton.

"I'm watching it now," she said as soon as she answered the phone.

The Real Housewives of Adverse City

"Can you believe someone killed Breyonna in prison, of all places? I mean, she hasn't been in Adverse City long enough for her to make enemies, especially while being locked up."

"You may find it hard to believe, but I sure don't. No telling how many enemies Breyonna made since being in this city. Apparently, someone on the inside of the jail hated her just as much as we did."

"I didn't hate her. I hated what she was dong to us, or should I say what she *did* to us."

"Exactly, which is why I'll say what you're probably thinking but since you're God's man, you feel you can't say it."

"Which is?" replied Carlton.

"Which is, I'm glad she's dead. She ruined my life and my son's life. I say, ding dong the wicked old witch is dead."

"Peyton, that's not a nice thing to say about Breyonna. She lost her life. She may have caused her share of trouble, but she had issues. She went through a lot."

"Yeah, yeah, we all have issues," Peyton said. "There was no excuse for what she did to us."

"I know that, but we're supposed to forgive if we want to be forgiven."

"Whatever, Carlton. You're paid to tell that to your congregation. Me, I'm no preacher, thank God. I'm just an ordinary person so I'll tell you what God loves to hear – and that's the truth."

"You're wrong, and you know it," Carlton said.

"Look, it's not Sunday, and you're not my preacher today. You're Liam's father and you of all people should be just as happy as I am that we don't have to worry about her and her big mouth any longer. Maybe now you can move on with your life. I know I am. I've got to get my family back."

Carlton listened as Peyton continued to express her satisfaction over Breyonna's death. He hated to admit it and would never say it out loud, but he felt the same way.

Peyton continued her chatter while Carlton remained quiet. When they finished talking and hung up the phone, he went online and replayed the news conference. As he leaned back in his office chair watching it, a subtle smile appeared on his face.

TO BE CONTINUED

Words from the Author

"Comfort and prosperity have never enriched the world as much as adversity has." Billy Graham

Everything was in turmoil in the lives of the housewives. Being rich could not shield them from problems and trouble. If anything, it may have increased it. Money couldn't buy or bring true satisfaction to any of them. All the riches in the world couldn't help them find what they most longed for – unconditional love, real happiness, and acceptance.

So much had happened in the lives of the housewives. Each woman struggled with the decisions they had made, some good and some not so good. They would have to reevaluate their lives and relationships. Their spiritual lives seemed to take a back seat when it came to making wise choices and seeking God's direction and guidance.

Such was the life of these four friends, "The Real Housewives of Adverse City." There is much more to learn about them and their drama fueled lives.

There still remains much unfinished business between Meesha and Carlton. She needed to clear her head so she packed up the boys and went to Los Angeles to visit relatives.

Avery was happier than she'd been in a very long time, and Carlton promised her that soon they would be able to tell everyone the truth about their relationship. She massaged her belly as she thought about sharing her baby news with the man she loved.

Peyton insisted to anyone who would listen that Meesha was wrong about her and Carlton's relationship. Peyton's excessive drinking seemed to escalate even though Breyonna was no longer a threat in her life.

Eva's dream of getting pregnant had come true but at an extremely high cost. Added to her situation was the recent ultrasound that revealed some startling and unexpected news.

Being ultra-rich and having the best of everything couldn't keep them from experiencing the mass trials and tribulations of the world. Such is life. Many times we think that if only we had material wealth and gain then we would somehow be shielded from hardship and hurt. However, that is not the way life always works. Money can never bring lasting happiness and complete satisfaction. It may seem like it can, at least for a while, but in reality that is not the case.

Peyton, Meesha, Avery, and Eva will have to learn that their great wealth, their relationships, marriages, all of it is for naught if they do not exercise humbleness, truthfulness, self-control and a reliance on God.

As I continue writing this series about "The Real Housewives of Adverse City," perhaps these four women will begin to understand that they should seek wisdom and spiritual insight. Only time will tell if they do!

"Whoever ignores instruction despises himself, but he who listens to reproof gains intelligence." Proverbs 15:32

Shelia E. Bell

Book Discussion Guide Questions

1. Who is your favorite character in "The Real Housewives of Adverse City?" Why?

2. Who is your least favorite character in "The Real Housewives of Adverse City?" Why?

3. Which housewife can you relate to the most, if any. In what way? Or why?

4. Was Peyton wrong for the manner in which her son came into her life? Would you have done the same thing?

5. What do you think about the husbands of the housewives?

6. What do you think about the title of this series and how does it tie in with the overall story?

7. Would life be worse if these women were not rich? Why or why not?

Additional titles by Shelia E. Bell
(Formerly Lipsey)

YA Titles
House of Cars
The Life of Payne

Series Novels
My Son's Wife (Book I)
My Son's Ex-Wife: The Aftermath (Book II)
My Son's Next Wife (Book III)
My Sister My Momma My Wife (Book IV)
My Wife My Baby and Him (Book V)
The McCoys of Holy Rock (Book VI)

Beautiful Ugly (Book I)
True Beauty (Book II)

Single Novels
Always, Now and Forever Love Hurts
Show A Little Love (out of print)
Into Each Life
Sinsatiable
Only In My Dreams

Anthologies
Learning to Love Me: Ordinary Women with
Extraordinary Stories
Weary & Will
Bended Knees (out of print)

For book events and
to arrange speaking and/or appearance
engagements with this author
Contact
www.sheliaebell.net
sheliawritesbooks@yahoo.com
Twitter and Instagram: @sheliaebell
www.facebook.com/sheliaebell

All Shelia E Bell (Lipsey) titles are available in
Print and eBook formats

Get more Info About Shelia E. Bell books!

CPSIA information can be obtained
at www.ICGtesting.com
Printed in the USA
LVOW07s1408300717

543157LV00002B/104/P